Mystery on Macomber Hill

(A Baker Boys Adventure)

John F. Balser Jr.

DEDICATION

This book is dedicated to my older brothers (Fred, David, Gordon, and Dean) who, as children, endured more of the poverty and hardships of living in (small town) Maine than I did. The good part is that we never knew it. It is also dedicated to Marcia, my favorite sister. Our family was full of love, caring, understanding and hard work. We were taught that there was always someone worse off than we could possibly be so we were more concerned about others than about ourselves. I also dedicate this book to my mother and father, Sarah and John Balser. Without them, my life would not have been such a joy!

CHAPTERS

Cats in the Cellar

It was 5:15 am on June 21st, the first day of summer, as the sun lifted its head up over Macomber Hill. The year was 1957. Josh Baker and his son Billy were already up and tending to their morning rituals.

Josh was the foreman for the Robinson dairy farm located atop 'The Hill' in North Jay, Maine. Two brothers, Everett and Carl Robinson, owned the dairy. They had taken over the operation several years back after their father had passed away. Everett was of normal stature, 5' 10", and 165 pounds, with grey/black hair. He was in his late 40's. His brother, Carl, was a few years younger, but much larger. He was a big man to begin with, but over the last five years he had become ill and added on about 100 pounds. He was now in the 400 pound range and smoked cigars like a chimney. He needed two canes to get about and always kept to himself. You hardly ever saw him out. Everett had taken over most of the responsibility of running the dairy.

Josh Baker and his wife, Sophie, lived in a farmhouse just down the road from the dairy. The Robinsons owned the house and its use was part of the contract with Josh when he accepted the position as foreman, about three years prior. Josh was tall, just over 6', with black hair and hazel eyes. He weighed in around 185 pounds and was solid as a rock. He had worked hard all his life and kept himself in good physical condition. No smoking and no drinking. He had a great sense of humor, a very strong Maine accent, and he loved Hank Williams music. He would be 35 years old this year.

Josh and Sophie had two sons, William (Billy) and Jacob (Jake). The only time they were called William and Jacob was when Sophie got upset or angry. Billy was born on February 2nd, in 1944. He was 13, tall and lean, with jet black hair. He had a mild disposition like his father and had just recently begun thinking about his future. Jake was born on April 22nd in 1946. He was 11, with a stocky build, and golden brown hair like his mother. He could be moody at times when things didn't suit him. How hard it would be for them to imagine that this particular summer would be etched in their minds forever.

As you drove towards North Jay, headed south from Wilton, Macomber Hill Road was on your left. It was about halfway between the two towns. The 'Hill', as it was called in the area, was a quiet and beautiful place. Down at the bottom, the train tracks crossed the road on their way south to Boston. As you started up the 'Hill', the Cutlers lived on the right, their house sitting a stone's throw from the tracks. Josh often wondered how they could stand being so close to the tracks.

The large fields, on both sides, continued up the hill. Broken stone walls and remnants of rusty old barb wire fencing bordered the road. The fields ambled up until you crested the 'Hill'. They had been cut, dried, and bailed just a week prior. They were once used for grazing, but the farm that had been there had burned years ago. Except for an opening in the stone wall on the right, there were no signs of its existence at all.

The house that the Bakers lived in was on the left at the end of the field. The gravel drive went straight in until you reach the barn. The house set sideways to the road, with the front facing the driveway. It had three sheds attached together on the right side, leading all the way out to where the third shed connected with the barn.

Two hundred feet past their driveway, on the right, was Mr. Edward Fitzpatrick's house. He was elderly and had been retired for many years. His wife had passed away a year earlier so he did very little socializing and spent most of his days, especially during the summer, working around his home. The house seemed so out of place in an area of mostly older farmhouses and shacks.

Josh would say to Sophie, "Looks like one a them homes in them fancy home magazines."

It was a small white ranch, exquisitely cared for, with a perfectly trimmed row of low hedges along the front next to the road. The grass on the front lawn was the thickest and greenest you would ever find, without a weed in sight. It was cut, trimmed and manicured to perfection. A small flower bed was located exactly in the center, lined with golden brown bricks that made it stand out even more. The driveway was trimmed on the left side by a long row of forsythia bushes that shot out golden yellow flowers in early spring that disappeared as quickly as they came. At the end of his driveway was a two-car garage, with an open breezeway in between, that attached to the home.

"Ain't nothin' like it round hea'," Josh would say.

More fields followed on both sides and then came the Robinson dairy. It sat atop the hill like a castle that perched upon a mountaintop in one of those European pictures. It was a large and stately old colonial home that sat near the front of the property facing the road. Two enormous oak trees, between it and the roadside, shot upwards toward the heavens and provided some much needed shade in the heat of summer. The gravel drive went in past a long porch on the right side of the house. It widened out into a circle as you approached the barns. There was a long storage shed on the right followed by the new garage. It had just been built to hold all the farm equipment.

The milk house sat straight ahead at the end of the circle drive. Inside the milk house was the newest equipment available. It held stainless steel coolers, tanks and hoses, and everything else needed to help modernize the processing of the milk The Robinsons were considered the biggest and best in the area and they maintained their business as such. Josh took great pride in keeping everything spotless.

He would always brag about it. "If ya don't get blinded by tha gleam than it ain't clean. It's gotta shine like tha sun at high noon in July."

The two red barns sat directly behind the milk house. They held 157 head of the healthiest Holsteins and Jersey dairy cows you could find anywhere. The Holsteins were black and white and were known for their outstanding milk production. The Jerseys were mostly cinnamon brown and produced a rich and creamy milk. At the left end of the barns were two back to back silos with bright silver tops towering into the sky like rocket ships ready to launch. The grazing pastures lay out behind the barns and seemed to stretch for miles. The Robinsons owned it all. The fields coming up the hill, Josh's house, and the grazing pastures, all leading right up to the dairy. They owned everything, except for the Fitzpatrick's home.

As you passed the dairy farm there were a few more homes along the way, as it slowly narrowed into a back road. A second road shot off to the left that lead to Beans Corner. That is where the Beans Corner Baptist Church was located. Josh and the family would head there every Sunday for a day of worship. If you took a right turn, you would head down Woodman Hill Road towards Jay Hill Road. A right turn at that intersection would then take you straight back into the center of North Jay. You would once again cross the train tracks just before coming to the four-way stop at the center of town.

At 6:45 am, Josh and Billy finished cleaning up after the morning milking and let the cows out to graze. They were headed across the circle drive towards the equipment garage. The boys were out of school for the summer and Billy would be working with his dad until school started back up in the fall. Jake helped to, but usually at home with his mother, rather than with his dad at the dairy. That would soon change, as he got a little older. Callie, the Robinson's calico cat, weaved in and out between Billy's legs as they walked from the barns to the garage. He had become her favorite ever since he started giving her that extra bowl of fresh milk every day.

Everett Robinson was just coming out of the porch, headed towards his car. "Mornin' Josh, how's everything goin'?"

"Mornin' Everett," Josh answered. "Everythins' fine, gittin' ready ta check out tha equipment."

4

"I gotta' head ta the bank in Farmington. Be back later." He waved to them as he hopped into his car, muttering something about balances and wrong numbers.

Billy looked at Josh. "What times Uncle Dave gonna' get here?"

"Oh, should be hea by suppa, he ain't leavin' Connecticut till bout ten aclock," Josh replied. "Ya motha's problee scurryin' round like a chicken with its head cut off," he chuckled. "She ain't seen her brotha' fa bout three years. Ya know she's gonna' have everything shipshape fa when he gits hea."

Billy was smiling as he pictured his mother prancing around the house, cooking and cleaning, like the headless horseman in the book he had just read in school. Callie took off back towards the barns as they entered the garage. It was at this time each year that Josh picked a day to inspect all the equipment, top to bottom. He had to make sure everything was ready for the next haying and harvesting. Today was that day.

As Billy entered the garage, he gazed up at the corn harvester that sat back in the corner. It was a large orange piece of machinery with a chute that shot up towards the top of the garage like a long giraffe's neck. The Robinsons leased two fields across town for growing cow corn. By early fall it would be harvested and transferred into the silos for winter feed. Billy closed his eyes and could imagine the intoxicating smell that exploded into the air as the shredded corn made its way into the silos.

"You nap'n?" Josh yelled from across the garage.

Billy quickly opened his eyes and walked over to where Josh was knee-deep into a tractor motor checking the hoses and wiring for any problems.

"Nope, I was just thinking about how much fun it is when they cut the corn and bring it in."

At that moment, Billy remembered a joke he had heard at school.

"Hey dad, you know why the ear of corn wanted to join the Army."

"Can't say as I do," said Josh.

"He wanted to be a kernel!" Billy started laughing.

Josh let out a bellow of laughter as he brought his head up and banged it against the side of the open motor cover.

"WOW," he said still laughing. "Sure hope tha rest of ya jokes don't hurt like that one."

Billy and Josh laughed some more before settling back down to work. They would spend the rest of the day inspecting all the equipment and making all necessary repairs. Josh would always explain what he was checking, any problems that he found, and how he was fixing it. Billy listened, eager to learn from his father.

Back at home, Sophie was in the kitchen preparing lunch. She was thin in stature, but not frail. She stood about 5'7". Her long golden brown hair fell below her shoulders but most of the time it was tied in a knot on the back of her head. Her features were beautiful in a plain sort of way. The tough farm life had not taken away the softness in her face.

She had just taken the fresh-baked bread out of the oven when she first heard the noise. It was a very faint scratching sound with no indication of where it was coming from. "Those darn cats," she thought to herself as she walked from the kitchen to the front doorway. "They're gonna' wreck that screen." The front door was already open as she peered out through the screen door. There was no sign of any cats. "Cleo, Moses, where are you," she called as she turned left and headed for the shed door. The string of sheds, three in all, attached to the right side of the house and took you all the way out to the hay barn. The barn was used to store extra hay for the dairy during the winter and it served as a place for the boys to play in, year-round.

As she opened the door and poked her head out into the first shed, she felt a slight breeze brush by her. Gazing around she could see the wood pile, a few of the boys toys scattered around, two rusty old sleds hanging on the back wall and a big rusty can of nails sitting on the floor. However, no cats! Peering out into the second shed, she could make out some of the chains hanging from the rafters. This was where Josh would be hanging the deer he would shoot this coming fall. She called once more for the cats, but seeing no activity, proceeded back to the kitchen to finish preparing lunch for Josh and the boys.

She started thinking about her brother and how wonderful it will be to see him again. It had been three years since David had moved to Connecticut with his new bride. Now, three years later, divorced, and no children, he was coming to stay with them for a while. "Thank God no kids," she mumbled. "It's always such a sad event especially when there's kids involved."

Dave was two years older than Sophie but they had always been very close growing up. She sure did miss him. He was a skilled mechanic and was leaving a good job to come back here to live. He had told Sophie that he had enough money saved to get him by for several months. She hoped that he would be able to relax and perhaps even find some work in the area. That would surely keep him close to her and he could stay with them until he could get a place of his own.

The screen door rattled opened as Josh and Billy entered the house. Lunchtime also serve as family time. It was a time when they could share information and talk about things that were going on that day. They would no doubt follow the same procedure when it came to supper time. Sophie gazed out from the kitchen, her thoughts were still about her brother.

"Where's Jake?" Billy asked.

Sophie came back to reality. "Oh, he's out back diggin' dandelion greens. I thought Uncle Dave might like some for supper. He probably ain't had any for years, and he always did love em."

Josh looked out into the kitchen. "Lunch ready?"

"Just about, you guys get washed up and I'll set the table." Sophie chirped.

"I'm going out back to get Jake." Billy darted out the screen door and ran around the corner of the house. "Hey Jake, where are you?"

"Right here," Jake yelled back just as Billy came around the corner. He was on his knees, a large kitchen fork in one hand and one of Sophie's cooking pots sitting next to him on the ground. There was a disgusted look on his face. Billy looked into the pot and smiled. It looked like more dirt than dandelion greens.

"How come you get to help dad all day and I have to stay here and dig weeds?"

Billy was still smiling. "You know you'll be able to help dad soon enough. Just need to get a little older."

"Can't wait for that," Jake replied.

"Come on, mom's got lunch ready and you know dad's gonna' want to get right back to the dairy when we're done. So let's go!"

Billy grabbed the pot as Jake got up and they scurried back towards the front. Billy was wondering what his mother was going to do with all of this dirt.

Josh had already seated himself at the table by the time they entered the house. "Wash up, en be quick bout it!"

Billy handed his other the pot and said, "Mostly dirt", in a low sarcastic voice as he headed for the sink.

"You hush William James. Your brother did a fine job gatherin' them greens and I'm sure we'll have a better supper because of it."

Jake looked at Billy and stuck out his tongue. Billy flicked the water from his hands into Jake's face. "Cut it out!" Jake whimpered.

Josh looked across the kitchen. "OKAY YOU TWO, git ova hea en sit – lunchtime! There's lots more work ta be done this afternoon."

Sophie said a quick grace, reached over and passed Josh a glass of milk. They all help themselves to the homemade chicken salad sandwiches made with Sophie's exquisite homemade bread. Josh would always tell her that she should try to sell it locally 'Cause it was soooo good'. She would laugh, call him silly, and then forget about it. A large bowl of potato salad accompanied the sandwiches.

Josh talked about the dairy and Jake had his standard everyday question, "When am I gonna' be able to help at the dairy?"

Josh would give his standard answer. "Soon as you're a little olda."

Sophie was flushed with excitement. "I'm so excited about David coming!"

"Dad said you were running around with no head, mom."

Josh looked at Billy with his eyes narrowed and his brow all wrinkled up. Sophie laughed, knowing exactly what he meant.

"I'm just so excited!"

Lunch was over, Josh and Billy headed back to the dairy and Sophie started clearing the table. Jake helped his mother take the dishes to the sink.

"Jake, go down cellar and get me two jars of tomatoes. They are right next to the green beans."

Sophie had outdone herself last fall. She had spent over two weeks cooking and canning every vegetable you could think of and they were all stored on the shelves Josh had put up for her in the cellar.

Jake pulled open the cellar door and reached up for the string that pulled the light on. He could still smell the faint odor from the wood furnace that blazed red in the dead of winter. It was mixed with the mustiness from the dark dampness of the cellar floor. As he pulled the string that wound through little islets till it reached the light, he could hear a scratching sound over near the back wall. As quick as he heard it, something hit his leg and he jumped back on the stairs. Cleo, a beautiful three colored cat, bounded up the stairs and through the cellar doorway. They had gotten her from a litter that belonged to Callie, the Robinsons calico barn cat. "Probably after them mice," Jake muttered as he headed towards the canned vegetables.

His eyes widened as he looked at the vast variety of jars that line the shelves. "Here they are," he said softly to himself as he pulled out the jar of tomatoes. Sophie heard his footsteps as he reached the top of the stairs.

"The light, don't forget the light, Jake."

He pulled the string and closed the cellar door. Jake handed Sophie the jar of tomatoes. "Here, mom."

"Oh Jake, I needed two jars. I thought I had said two. Go grab me another one."

Jake curled his face up, drops his shoulders and let out a big sigh.

"Now Jacob, let's not get all huffy. We can't let Uncle Dave go hungry now can we. Besides, I'm making your favorite, - meatloaf!"

His expression lightened as he opened the cellar door, pull the light on, and headed back down the cellar stairs. Both cats, Cleo and Moses, darted down the steps as he headed for the tomatoes. As he pulled another jar from the shelf, he heard the scratching again.

"What are they doing?" He thought. He walked back towards the steps and on past the wood furnace.

Once his eyes cleared, the light allowed him to see almost everything around the cellar. It was a dim light and the back corners of the cellar were still darkened. He could see the outline of the cats near the corner scratching at the base of the rock wall. As he got closer, he bent down to shoo the cats out of the cellar. In the semi darkness, hc reached out to support himself against the jagged rocks that made up the cellar walls. As he grabbed hold of one of the rocks, it loosens and fell and he slipped down onto his knees. Jake set the jar of tomatoes down, turned, and looked up at the wall. He could see an opening where the stone had jarred loose. There was something in it! He reached in and extracted a small jar about 6 inches long. With the dim light, Jake couldn't tell, but it looks like there was a small piece of paper rolled up inside the jar. Jake was just starting to get excited when he heard his mother at the top of the stairs.

"Jake, what's taking you so long down there?"

"It's okay mom, I'm just trying to get Cleo and Moses outta here. They've been down here scratchin' at the walls."

Sophie remembered the scratching she had heard earlier. "Crazy cats," she mumbled to herself. "All right now, hurry up with them tomatoes and don't forget the light!"

Jake pushed the jar back into the opening and reached down for the loose rock. It slid right back in as if it had never fallen out. Thoughts of buried treasure and spies were rumbling through his mind. What could it be? He couldn't tell anyone about it, except Billy. Billy was older and would know what to do. Jake grabbed the tomatoes and headed for the stairs. His entire insides were shaking with excitement. He reached the string, gave it a quick yank, and headed out into the kitchen.

Sophie was shaking the dirt out of the dandelion greens as Jake closed the cellar door, walked over, and put the second jar of tomatoes on the counter. "Thank you, Jake. You're a great helper." She never turned to look at him or she would have seen the excitement in his eyes.

"Mom, can I go play now?" Jake asked.

"Sure, just stay within callin' distance in case I need some more help."

"Okay mom," Jake said as he raced out the front, the screen door slamming shut behind him.

His heart was racing a million miles an hour. What would he do for the rest of the afternoon? It would be forever before Billy gets home. He jumped up on the old stump that sat in the middle of the front yard. Sitting cross legged, he gazed out past the barn toward Spruce Mountain looming about a mile or so away.

Uncle Dave

Spruce Mountain was rightly named. It was covered with towering spruce trees, from top to bottom. They stretched across the breath of the mountain and proceeded upward. They became smaller and less entwined as you approached the top mixing in with the rocks and ledge. About three quarters of the way up, on the side facing the farm, was a large open field about 2 acres in size. Although looking quite small, you could see the open area from the house. Josh had come across the area while out deer hunting two years prior.

Upon further inspection of the area, he discovered that it contained the largest wild blueberry patch he had ever seen. He and the boys would go there often, when the berries were in season, and bring home buckets full for Sophie. She could always find plenty of uses for them. Pancakes, muffins, pies, cakes, – her list was endless. Whatever she didn't use up would be canned and put in the cellar for use during the winter.

The mountain was home to many beautiful deer, and Josh usually got one each year. It was a good little walk from the house to the mountain. You would have to go past the barn, through the fields, and across the grazing pasture. You would hit a small stand of timber, cross the brook and follow the wood trails and logging roads until you reach the base of the mountain.

During last trip, Josh let Billy lead the entire way to the mountain and back home. That was his way of making sure that Billy could get to and from the berry patch without getting lost. Upon arriving home he had taken Billy aside and told him, "Tha next time you en Jake go pickin', ya kin go without me". This was his way of telling Billy that he could depend on him.

"Don't worry bout ya motha'. I'll take care a that when tha time comes. "Billy had felt so grown up. It was the biggest responsibility that his father had ever given him. At supper that evening, right out of the blue, Josh had said, "I told Billy that tha next time they go berry pickin', they kin go without me."

Time stopped for a moment and there was a dead silence as all eyes were on Sophie. She looked nervously around the table and mumbled, "We'll see, we'll see." It was a done deal.

Sophie had spent the afternoon cleaning around the house and getting everything ready for supper and Dave's arrival. Jake came in about mid-afternoon to help her then he retreated to his room to play. She noticed that he was acting kind of strange, fidgety and nervously excited, but she paid it no mind.

When she heard the pickup truck pull into the drive, she glanced quickly at the clock in the kitchen. It was a big old rooster clock that Josh had bought over at Woolworth's in Farmington. It was 5:15 pm.

"Oh my God, he's here! Jake, Jake, get down here, Uncle David is here!"

She pressed her hands into her cheeks to try to add a little color. In a quick motion, she undid her apron and tossed it over the back of the couch. She brushed down the front of her dress with both hands and rushed towards the screen door. Jake came running down from upstairs and was right behind her as they entered the yard.

David Clough turned off the engine, swung the door open, and stepped out onto the gravel driveway. He dropped his cigarette and crushed it under the toe of his shoe. He was a lanky sort, around 6'2", with golden brown hair just like Sophie's. He was a good-looking man at the age of 36 and ready to start a new life. He was grinning ear to ear as Sophie flew into his arms, almost knocking him back against the green pickup truck.

"David, Oh David!" Sophie was crying as she flung her arms around his neck. Cannonball tears were rushing down her cheeks. She kissed him fiercely on the side of his face. "I've missed you so much. It seems like forever since we've seen each other."

Dave was squeezing Sophie with both of his arms wrapped around her waist.

"Ah, my little Soph, I've missed you too. It's so great to be here!" He always called her that when they were growing up in Wilton. It had always made her feel safe and secure with her older brother around.

Jake noticed a slight misty look in Uncle Dave's eyes, but he wasn't crying.

"Hi, Uncle Dave."

Sophie released her grip on her brother and moved around to his side with her arm around his waist.

"David, look how much Jake has grown since the last time you saw him. He's eleven now, he was only eight then."

Dave pulled his arm down from around Sophie's shoulders and extended his hand out to Jake.

"Well, you certainly have grown into a fine young man, and a handsome one, too!"

"Thanks," was his shy reply.

Jake was smiling inside. Uncle Dave had just called him a 'man'. Maybe now dad would let him start helping out at the dairy.

Sophie grabbed Dave's hand. "Let's go inside. We can get your things brought in later when Josh and Billy get home. They should be here in an hour or so as soon as the late milking is done."

They strolled inside and Jake took up a position in Josh's stuffed chair. Sophie and Dave sat together on the couch. They talked for a bit about the farm, Connecticut, and other catch-up conversation. Sophie got up and headed to the kitchen to get supper ready. Dave swung his long legs over the end of the couch and laid his head back on the other end.

"Think I'll rest for a while, it was a long drive."

Jake headed upstairs with thoughts of his secret discovery springing back into his mind.

It was 6:15 pm when Josh and Billy headed down the road towards home. Mr. Fitzpatrick was in his yard, picking and plucking around the edge of the lawn. He hated weeds and spent hours making sure there weren't any growing in his yard.

"How ya doin', Ed," Josh shouted from across the road.

Mr. Fitzpatrick pulled himself upright on his knees and tipped his head back so that he could see out from under the big straw hat he always wore while working in the sun.

"Josh, Billy," he acknowledged with a nod, as he made a grunting noise and stood up. He was short and stocky and spoke with a deep gravelly voice. "Fourth of July is just around the corner. Don't forget to get over here for the festivities."

"Sure we ain't gonna' forgit," Josh yelled back.

Mr. Fitzpatrick was an odd old man and never talked much, but every year on the Fourth of July, he put on the biggest and best fireworks display right in his own backyard. Josh could never understand how he got away with it since it was illegal to have them. Nevertheless, every year everyone on the 'Hill' would gather in the backyard of this pristine little white house and enjoy the show. Mr. Fitzpatrick had told Josh that he always called the police every year to tell them not to come up the hill on the night of the Fourth of July. "If they don't see anything, they won't have anything to be concerned about," he always told Josh. Josh figured he must have some kind of connection with the county officials.

They exchanged "see you later's" as Josh and Billy proceeded towards home. As they approached the driveway, Billy caught a glimpse of the green pickup truck parked next to Josh's black Pontiac.

"Dad, Uncle Dave's here!"

Billy bounded up the drive, headed for the front door. He swung open the screen door and rushed into the living room.

"Uncle Dave!"

Dave looked up at Billy through squinted eyes as he pulled his legs off the end of the couch and sat up. His nap was over. Billy was standing right in front of him as he wiped his eyes to bring things into focus. Dave extended his hand out towards Billy.

"Hey, Billy. You've grown about two feet since I saw you last."

"Sure have," Billy replied, "and I've been helping dad at the dairy this year."

The screen door shut with its usual bang, as Josh entered the house. Sophie had come out around from the kitchen and Jake had scurried down from upstairs as Josh entered the room. Dave stood up quickly from the couch and walked towards him, his hand outstretched.

"Josh, it's been a while. It's great to see you again."

Josh clasped Dave's hand and right shoulder at the same time. "Same hea. Ya ain't changed none. Just git hea?"

"No, about quarter past five. I took a little nap while Soph was getting supper ready. The drive made me a little tired."

"Well, you're a welcome sight. Sophie's been runnin' round all day gittin' things ready."

"Without her head!" Billy yelled from across the room.

They all laughed. Sophie headed back towards the kitchen. "Billy, you and Jake get washed up. You two can help me set supper."

Josh took up residence in his favorite stuffed chair. Dave walked over and sat back down on the couch and yawned. He was still tired from the long drive. As they chatted, Sophie and the boys prepared the table.

"Supper's ready," came the call from the kitchen.

And what a supper it was! They hadn't seen anything like this since last Thanksgiving. The fancy dishes were out, all matching, with little patterns of roses and vines swirling throughout each piece. A single candle sat in the middle of the table twinkling as the flame moved from side to side. Sophie had really outdone herself with this one. The smell of the fresh-baked buns filled the room as she opened the oven door. She immediately took charge.

"Everyone set. David, your place is right here," as she pointed to the right side of the table. He was seated directly across from the boys with Josh and Sophie to his left and right.

The large meatloaf, made extra special with the canned tomatoes, freshly chopped scallions, and breadcrumbs, sat in the center of the table next to the candle. It was surrounded by a heaping bowl of mashed potatoes, gravy, and a variety of smaller bowls that held all the vegetables – squash, peas, and fresh carrots. She sat the fresh-baked buns on the edge of the table and sat down.

"Could we all join hands, I'd like to say grace." They all join hands to form an unbroken ring around the table.

"Dear God, we'd like to thank you for helpin' David arrive safely and for all the blessin's that you have given us as a family. Thanks for the food that we are about to share. We know that there are many in this world that are not as fortunate as we are. In Jesus name – Amen." They all echoed in with "Amen".

Now it was time to eat. There was one special bowl, still covered, sitting in front of Dave." David, could you take the cover off that," Sophie said solemnly, as she pointed to the bowl.

"Sure thing!" He reached for the cover and lifted it as a puff of steam slowly rose upward from the bowl. "Oh my gosh!"

Dave exclaimed as he sat back in his chair staring at the bowl. "Greens! I haven't had greens since I left here three years ago... Soph, you are something!"

Her face was gleaming from his delight. Josh and the boys were smiling too.

"Jake dug em this mornin', just for you."

Dave set the cover down, looked across the table at Jake, and gave him a big wink. At the same time, he gave him the thumbs-up sign. With all that has happened recently, Dave thought how great it was going to be to get a fresh start and be with people who cared about him.

Supper brought conversation about a multitude of topics. Things like, Sophie and Dave growing up, the dairy, school, the Fourth of July, and general discussion about things that had happened over the past several years. It finally ended, and while Jake helped his mother clear the table, Josh and Billy were helping Dave bring in his belongings from the truck. He would be staying in Billy's room for the time being. Jake and Billy would be sharing Jake's room while Dave was here. Josh had moved Billy's bed down to Jake's room and set up a slightly larger bed for Dave.

It was approaching 9 pm. Billy and Jake headed upstairs and after quick baths, were ready for bed. Sophie, Josh and Dave all came in to say good night. Sophie said the quick "Now I lay me" prayer with the boys and then she headed back downstairs.

"Nite, boys."

"Nite ,mom," Billy said.

"Nite," Jake echoed.

Sophie turned the light off and closed the door. Jake waited a few seconds as his excitement started building. In a whisper he said, "Billy, Billy." He slid out of bed, walked over and sat down on the edge of Billy's bed. "You're gonna' get us in trouble if mom catches you out of bed," Billy muttered, his face buried deep inside his pillow. "Go to bed!"

"I found something today! It's like a treasure map or something. It was in the cellar."

Billy rolled over towards Jake and propped his head up on his elbow. "

What are you talking about?"

Jake couldn't hold it in. Everything came out at once. "I had to go to the cellar for mom – The cats were diggin' at the rock wall – I went to shoo them out and hit the wall –The rock fell out and I found a jar   – It looks like it has papers inside – Maybe it's some kind of treasure map or spy stuff, I ain't looked at it yet – I wanted to tell you so you could help me get it later!"

Billy put his finger to his lips. "Slow down. Mom will hear you. Tell me what happened...slower."

Jake took his time and repeated what had happened earlier in the day. Billy was starting to take interest in what he was hearing, although he had nowhere near the excitement that Jake had.

"Maybe dad put it there," Billy whispered.

"Don't think so. It was covered with dust and plenty rusty. Looked like it was there for a long time."

"Okay," Billy said. "We'll have to figure out how to get it up here so we can look at it. We should tell dad about it!"

Jake sat pouting on the edge of the bed. "Please don't tell yet. What if it really is some kind of treasure? Maybe we can find out first, please!"

"Yeah, yeah, I hafta help dad tomorrow. I gotta get to sleep. Go to bed and we'll see if we can get it up here later." Billy gave Jake a little push to help him along.

Jake crawled back under the covers as his thoughts led him into a night of adventurous dreams.

LETTERS AND NUMBERS

It was several days before an opportunity came about to retrieve Jake's discovery. Josh and Billy were at the dairy. Dave had gotten settled in and made it clear to Josh that he wanted to help earn his keep while he was here. There were a lot of handyman chores that needed to be done around the house. Dave assured Josh that he would see to it that they got done. He asked Josh to help him make a list of things. It included cutting the grass, fixing anything that was broken, helping in the vegetable garden, and starting to fill the woodshed and chop wood for the winter. Josh was delighted with Dave's help and energy. "Never too early ta git tha wood in. Then cold nights gonna' be hea fore ya know it," Josh had told Dave.

Dave just finished tightening the latch on the screen door. "Soph," he yelled. "I'm headed down to town. I gotta' get some gas and smokes. You need anything?"

"Not today," came the reply from inside the house.

"I should be back in a bit," he said as he climbed into the pickup. He backed out of the drive in his truck and slowly disappeared down the hill.

Sophie had just finished washing some clothes. She plopped them in a basket to take outside wish he would hang them to dry. Josh had put up new T – bars and restrung the clothesline last week. It was set up just past the big stump on the front lawn. Jake was sitting on the couch.

"Jake, could you fetch me some yellow beans for supper? I've gotta get these clothes hung out."

Jake's eyes lit up. "Sure mom." He yanked on the light and headed down the cellar stairs as Sophie scooped up the basket and headed for the door." Should have just enough time," he thought as he rushed over to the corner of the cellar.

With a quick pull, the stone came out of the wall and he set it down on the dirt floor. He reached in and extracted the jar, carefully tucked it into his shirt and headed for the shelves, almost tripping over the edge of the cement slab that held the furnace. He found the yellow beans and headed back up the stairs. With a quick flick the light was out. He sped out into the kitchen and put the beans on the counter. Holding the jar under his shirt, he raced upstairs to the bedroom. Once in the room, he crossed over to the dresser that sat against the wall between the two beds. Dropping to his knees, he pulled the bottom drawer completely out. He slipped the jar out of his shirt, placed it on the floor at the bottom of the dresser, slid the drawer back in, and took a big breath of air. Success! Now all he had to do was wait until tonight when he and Billy would finally get a look at it.

He hurried downstairs and out through the screen door and onto the gravel driveway. His face felt hot and flushed from all the running. His mother was still hanging out the clothes. Sophie looked over at him, smiling, but didn't say anything, totally unaware of what had just taken place. Dave returned later in the afternoon and spent the rest of the day working around the outside of the house.

Supper came and went, and it was soon time for bed. After their traditional good nights, Sophie turn the light out and closed the door to the boys room.

"I did it!" Jake whispered with excitement.

"Did what?"

"I got the jar from the cellar today!" His excitement was mounting.

"Where is it? Did you bring it up here?" Billy asked.

"Yup." Jake said as he quietly dropped his feet to the floor, moved toward the dresser and knelt down. "Want to see it?"

"What do you think?" Billy questioned sarcastically as he set up on the edge of his bed. "You gotta' be quiet or we'll be in big trouble."

Jake slid the bottom drawer out and removed the jar from its hiding place. He handed it to Billy. "See I told you," he whispered.

The jar was dusty with a rusty screw top cover, but after a few tries Billy was able to break it free and it started to open. He set the cover on the top edge of the dresser. "Can't see too good," he mumbled. He moved towards the window and pulled the curtain aside. It had been clouding up to rain earlier in the evening but for now the large yellow moon flooded the room with a soft golden glow. Billy held the jar by the bottom tipped it up and shook it gently. The rolled up paper slid partway out of the top. He grasped the paper with two fingers and gently removed it from the jar. He placed the jar next to the cover on the dresser.

"Let me see! Let me see!" Jake yelled in a whispered voice. A cloud had passed across the moon and the room had darkened.

"Hold on a second," Billy said, putting his finger up toward Jake. "We need more light." The cloud crept slowly by, and finally the moonlight darted back into the room.

Billy and Jake knelt in front of the window sill. Billy flattened the paper out on the sill and they both looked at it.

"What's it say?" Jake asked. "Is it a map? What is it?"

"Quiet!" whispered Billy as he studied the paper. The paper was small, about 3" x 5". An inch down in the middle was printed the word – SHARE. Below that were three lines of letters and numbers. First was SG – 35, second was FW – 35, and the third line was TINY – 30 written across the bottom separated from the other three lines was the following: ST – 2 LEFT SIDE. That was it? Nothing made any sense to the boys as they knelt there, staring at the paper.

SHARE

SG – 35

FW – 35

TINY – 30

ST–2   LEFT SIDE

"Got nothin' on it that makes any sense," said Billy as he slid it closer to Jake.

"Just some letters and numbers and a couple of words."

Jake had a disappointing look on his face. His dreams of buried treasure and spies were fading away fast. "Just a bunch of dumb letters," he muttered discouragingly.

"We'll look at it tomorrow." Billy said. "I don't have to work with dad for a while. Mr. Robinson hired a couple of new guys to help out at the farm. I'll tell you about it tomorrow. We better get to bed before they hear us." Billy picked up the jar, screwed the cover back on and opened the window high enough to throw the jar out towards the backyard. "Uncle Dave will find it and throw it away," he thought. He closed the window, pulled the curtain, folded the paper in half and placed it in the corner of the top drawer. Jake had replaced the bottom drawer and was already in bed.

Billy hopped back into bed and slid down under the cover. He laid back on his pillow, his arms folded back, with his hands under his head. As he gazed at the far wall, he could see the small rays of moonlight as they squeezed their way in through the cracks in the curtains. He lay like that for a while, letting the letters and numbers run through his head. What could they mean? Probably nothin'! He would check them out again tomorrow. He could hear Jake's heavy breathing as he drifted off to sleep.

Sophie had switched off the boys light and headed back down to the living room for coffee. When she reached the bottom of the stairs, she could hear Jack Benny on the radio saying, 'ROCHESTER', as he did so many times throughout his shows. Josh and Dave were both laughing as she walked in and sat down on the couch. Josh reached over, turned off the radio and said, "I was just tellin' Dave bout what happened taday at tha barn. Everett came by durin' milkin' with two new men he'd hired, Fred and Skip. Seems they're gonna' be there for a spell, with hayin' and harvestin' comin' up. Plus, then two fellows will be helpin' me in tha barns."

"Oh, that's wonderful, Josh." Sophie said smiling ear to ear. "You work so hard, it's about time they got you some help."

"Yep, I'm tha best," he said boastingly, poking his chest out, "But it'll sure be nice ta have some more help. I told Billy he didn't have ta help for a while. He needs ta have some summa, though he's never complained bout helpin'. He sure is a good one!"

"They both are," Dave chipped in.

"Yup, think I'll keep em." Josh and Dave both chuckled while Sophie wrinkled up her mouth and shook her head.

"Well," said Dave. "I heard an interesting story today about this very house you live in. I stopped by the grain store to pick up some smokes and got talking with George. He said to say hi, by the way."

"George was always a talka," Josh broke in.

Dave smiled. "Anyway, I was telling him how I had just come up here from Connecticut to stay with you for a while. Do you remember back about ten or eleven years ago when we were all living over in Wilton? There was a string of bank robberies over through Farmington and all the way down to Livermore."

"Oh, I remember that," Sophie said. "It was right around the time Jake was born."

"Yup, I remember it too," Josh acknowledged.

Dave continued his story. "This house had been empty for a year or so. Well, it seemed that a few days after the last robbery, the older couple that lived across the street noticed some men going in and out of the house after dark."

"The Fitzpatricks'?" Josh interrupted.

"Yeah, I think that's the name. He said the old man called the cops and before you knew it, there was a shootout going on. Both of them fellows were killed but not before they had shot one of the cops. They found some of the money bags from the banks and a few bills when they checked the bodies. Other than that, none of the money from the robberies was ever found. George said there's always been talk about a third man, probably the driver because they always got away from the bank so fast, but there was never any evidence to prove it. The old man got word that the cop had been shot and he fixed him up some kind of a bandage and a tourniquet. The doctor said that the cop would have bled to death if the old man hadn't fixed him up. Those two fellows, Sam Green and Frank Walker, had grown up right in this area and used to work for the Robinson's farm."

"Isn't that something," Sophie said, gazing at Dave in amazement.

Josh leaned back in his big stuffed chair. "I remember hearin' bout all that stuff. Never knew it was this place."

"Yup, I guess it's pretty famous here on the 'Hill'," Dave concluded.

Josh started to get up from his chair. "Only thing famous round these parts, are then damn black flies." He and Dave laughed.

"Josh Baker, such language!" Sophie said as she shot a scolding look at him. "I'm headed to bed."

"Me too," Josh said. "Gittin' late en mornin' comes mighty early."

Sophie was already sleeping by the time Josh finished his bath and climbed into bed. He was still thinking about Dave's story. Now he knew why the police never bothered Mr.

Fitzpatrick when he put on his Fourth of July display. He glanced over at Sophie. She always had such a calm and beautiful look about her. He smiled as he laid his head back onto the pillow and drifted off to sleep.

The Fishing Trip

"Think I'll go fishing today," Billy thought, as he propped himself up in bed. It was 7:00 am. He hadn't slept this late for quite a while and he felt refreshed and wide awake. He jumped out of bed and quickly dressed. As he grabbed a pair of socks of the top dresser drawer, he remembered the paper. He slid it out of the corner and slipped it into his pants pocket. He and Jake could check it out again later. He threw on his socks, grabbed his sneakers and headed out the door to go down to the kitchen. Jake was already dressed and seated at the table when Billy came around the corner.

"Just in time," Sophie said smiling. "Since it's your first mornin' home in a while, I made you a special breakfast – Blueberry Pancakes!"

Billy's eyes lit up. This was great! No work, a special breakfast, what more could he asked for. It was going to be a great day. After breakfast, the boys help Sophie clear the table. "I was thinkin' of goin' fishin' today, mom. Maybe I could get some nice "brookies" for supper."

"It rained some during the night and it's supposed to rain again today," was her response.

"That's okay," said Billy. "I'll get back quick if it looks like a bad one. I'm just goin' down to the brook past the pasture. Can Jake go with me?"

"On one condition," Sophie said, in her, you – had – better – do – as – I – say, voice. "You promise not to go no further than that brook and if the weather starts lookin' bad, you get right back here."

"Promise," said Billy.

"Promise!" yelled Jake, as he dropped the silverware in the sink. "Thanks mom." He walked over and hugged her around the waist.

Billy grabbed a small paper bag and a coffee can from under the sink. They headed out to the shed closest the barn to fetch the fishing poles and gear. They packed the bag with fishing line, sinkers and hooks. Billy handed Jake the coffee can as he ran back to the second shed to get a shovel. He returned in an instant and they headed out towards the vegetable garden behind the barn. The best place for worms was right along the edge of the garden. They dug enough worms in about ten minutes to last them all day. Sophie was standing in the doorway when they came around the side of the barn to put the shovel away. Billy tossed it back into the shed, and looked at his mother.

"We're leaving now, mom."

"Okay, Billy, you be careful and remember what I said."

"We will. See ya."

They waved to her and headed out past the garden, veered off to the right, and into the field. Sophie leaned against the door sill thinking about how fast they had grown up and how it wouldn't be long before they will be worrying about kids of their own. It was a fairly short walk until you hit the grazing pasture. Billy and Jake were swatting at the black flies as they trudged along.

"I brought the paper with me," said Billy.

"What paper?" Jake had already forgotten about his big discovery.

"You know, the one from last night."

"Oh yeah, don't make no sense to me.

"I figured we could check it out again while we were down at the brook."

"Okay," Jake replied. His excitement about buried treasure and spies had faded fast.

Miles of barbwire fencing surrounded the two grazing pastures. There were three strands of wire with wooden fence posts about every 12 feet. In reality it was only one big field with the barbwire fencing running directly down the middle. It was Everett Robinson's idea. He said it gave each pasture time to re-vegetate and make it better for the cows. He would always joke with Billy about dumping truckloads of chocolate in one pasture, and keeping the grass in the other. This way, he could sell chocolate milk one week and regular milk the next. Billy smiled to himself as he thought about it. There were clouds in the sky but they didn't stop the intense warmth of this June day. As the boys approached the fencing, Billy noticed the stretch of dark clouds off in the distance. Jake knelt down by the fence and slid his fishing gear under the barbwire. Billy handed Jake his gear, and it joined Jake's on the other side.

"You go first," Billy said, as he grabbed the bottom strand of barbwire and pulled it up. The wire bowed upward and created a wider opening to crawl under. "Be careful, you know how sharp this stuff is."

Jake laid his body flat on the ground alongside the fencing and rolled to the other side. Once there, he stood up and took the wire from where Billy was holding it. "Go ahead, I got it."

Billy followed the same procedure and once they were safely on the other side, they picked up their gear and headed down across the pasture. Jake was looking around nervously, hoping the cows were in the other pasture today. He didn't like it when they were roaming around loose. It always seemed to bother him. Billy gave it no mind, one way or the other. There were no cows in sight today. "Sure is hot," Jake said.

"Won't be for long," Billy replied. "Rains comin' later. Should help cool it right off."

"Did you meet the new guys at the dairy yet?" Jake asked Billy as they walked through the pasture.

"Yup. Skip and Fred. Mr. Robinson brought them out to the barns last night while we were milkin'. He wanted to introduce them and show them around the barns. They're gonna' be helpin' dad quite a bit, till fall. I guess they're gonna' live right there with the Robinsons in a couple of rooms upstairs."

Jake kicked along at the ground as his voice saddened. "I ain't never gonna' get to help dad. Specially now with them new guys comin' in."

"Probably next year," Billy replied, trying to reassure Jake. "Dad let me start helpin' when I was twelve and you're gonna' be twelve pretty soon. Besides, I kind of like not havin' to go in this time of year."

Jake looked at Billy with an are you crazy look. He couldn't wait until it was his time to go help his dad.

Spruce Mountain loomed up in front of them as they approached the fencing on the back side of the pasture. Billy thought of what his dad had said about him and Jake goin' berry picking by themselves. The dark clouds were still some distance away, but getting closer. They proceeded under the fence with the same ritual as when they entered. They crossed through a small stand of timber and could hear the gurgling sound of running water as they approached the brook.

It had been an extremely hard winter and a rainy spring. The water was running much faster than normal for this time of year. As they reached the bank of the brook, Billy looked upstream to the spot where they usually crossed when they were on their way to the mountain. The brook was about thirty feet wide and a foot or so above normal. He could only see a few of the larger rocks that they use to get across. The rest were still hidden underwater. A couple of years ago, a very large tree had fallen straight across the brook. They could always use it as an alternative to get across, but it was quite a distance upstream. Using the rocks was much easier and quicker.

"I hope the water's down by the time we go berry pickin', or we're gonna' have to go way upstream to that big tree to cross."

Jake shook his head in agreement. Billy sat the can of worms down on a flat rock, dug in and pulled out two nice ones. He tossed one to Jake and they threaded them onto their respective hooks. They were ready to catch supper. Billy pointed downstream to a spot where the water slowed and spread out into a deep pool. A huge tree arched out over the pool as if it were ready to dive in. They picked up everything and moved about 30 feet downstream.

Jake was the first to cast and his line dropped about halfway out into the pool. "Nice," he thought as he sat down on the bank.

Billy was standing on a big rock right next to the bank. He threw his line out and it sailed past Jake's and landed right under the big tree in the middle of the pool. It was just where he wanted it. Josh had always preached patience to the boys when it came to fishing. Throw out your line, let it sink, and then sit and wait and wait and wait. Billy was okay with that concept and practiced it all the time. Jake, on the other hand, would have nothing to do with the idea. He would throw his line out, wait thirty seconds or so and reel it in. He could continue that process for hours. After he did it six or seven times, Billy said, "let it sit. They ain't gonna' bite if you keep yankin' it in."

"I know how to do it," Jake spouted back in a sarcastic tone.

Wouldn't you know, Jake was the first to hook one! It grabbed his hook the second the worm hit the water. "I got one!" Jake yelled.

"I don't believe-Whoa!" Billy shouted feeling a quick pull on his line. "I think I got one too."

Each had hooked a nice trout. They watch them darting side to side, trying to release themselves from the line. It was like a tug-of-war, man against fish. They slowly reeled them in and brought them up onto the bank. Jake placed his foot lightly on the side of his fish, bent down, and removed the hook from its lip. Billy's fish had taken the hook a little deeper. He held his around the middle and spread its mouth open wide. He had to reach his fingers into the mouth of the fish in order to grasp the hook and pull it out. Both fish were keepers. Billy looked around for a tree branch that he could use as a stringer. After finding one, he came back and ran the branch up through the gills of both fish and let them slide down onto the branch. A small "Y" on the other end kept them from falling off. "This is great," Billy said. They quickly added new worms to their hooks and got their lines back into the water. Billy had gone back to the rock. He reached down and took the paper out of his pocket, stepped back onto the bank, and set his pole down. "Wanna look at this?" He said as he waved the paper in the air at Jake.

"Yeah, okay," came the reply.

Jake set his pole down as Billy came over next to him. They sat there on the bank looking once again at the paper, trying to make some sense of it. "I wonder if it's a combination." Billy turned the paper in every direction. S2 Left Side, what could that last line mean? They kept looking at it and coming up with words and letters that really had no meaning at all. Jake got tired of it, stood up with his pole and started casting again. Billy sat there just staring at it. "There's got to be an answer to it," he thought.

Jake started yelling. "I got another one!"

Billy looked up as Jake started reeling in his line. It was another nice one. They were up to three. Billy put the paperback in his pocket and stood up. He could hear a slight rumble of thunder off in the distance. "Can't stay much longer. Sounds like the storm's gittin' closer. We should be outta here before long." They caught two more fish, five in all. It was just enough for a good supper.

"Okay Jake, let's go." It was starting to darken overhead. Jake didn't argue. They reeled in their lines, gathered up all their gear, and headed back. Billy carried the fish, all hanging motionless at the end of his stringer branch. Both were starting to get hungry. As they started back across the pasture, Jake could see the cows far off to the left. "Oh great," he mumbled softly. He made sure that he stayed right beside Billy as they walked across the pasture, constantly turning his head to make sure the cows were not coming towards them. Just as they crossed under the barbwire from the pasture and into the field, the sky opened up. The rain came down so heavy and fast that it hurt when it hit their faces. The sky was a swirling mass of black clouds. Then out of nowhere came flashes of jagged light that lit up the entire area. In an instant it was gone. They broke into a run across the field as the pounding rumble of thunder echoed around them. Jake was the first to reach the barn, Billy was right behind him. He had never seen Jake run so fast. They ducked into the barn and proceeded through the sheds to the living room door, laughing all the way at the sounds the water made inside their sneakers. They were drenched – head to toe.

Jake opened the door and poked his head in. "Mom, hey, mom, we're back!"

Sophie dropped her sewing, jumped up from the couch and came quickly to the doorway. As she looked out into the shed, she couldn't help but start laughing. There they were, standing side-by-side, both grinning and Billy holding up the fish. Their hair was matted down on their heads with water running down their faces and dripping from the ends of their chins. "You two look like a couple of drowned rats." Her laughter continued.

Both of the boys broke into laughter along with Sophie. "We almost made it," Billy said, wiping the water out of his eyes.

"Okay, let me have the fish. The two of you wait right here. I'm gonna' get some towels and dry clothes." She took the fish from Billy, headed for the kitchen, and dropped them in the sink. Hurriedly she went upstairs, grabbed some underwear and pants and hit the bathroom on the way by for two big towels. She was back at the shed door in no time. She stepped out into the shed with the boys. "You can dry off and change right out here," she said, as she handed them the towels. She'd tossed their clothes onto the wood pile. "Leave everything out here to dry. Don't need you trackin' all that wet into the house." The boys stripped down, dried themselves off and threw on the clothes that their mother had gotten for them. They grabbed all the wet clothes and hung them on nails along the wall of the shed. When they entered the house, they were still laughing, but much drier.

Sophie had returned to the couch to finish mending a couple of Josh's shirts. "Go fetch some shirts and socks then get down here. You need to get them fish out of the sink and clean them."

The boys made a beeline for their room to get the shirts and socks. Billy returned a few minutes later and headed into the kitchen.

"Where's Jake?" Sophie asked.

"Still upstairs. I'm gonna' clean the fish." He walked over and pulled out some newspaper from alongside the refrigerator. He carefully laid it out on the counter, picked up the stringer of fish and tipped them up over the paper. They slid off the top and onto the newspaper.

"Throw that stick out with everything else. Don't need that stuff smellin' up the house."

"Okay." Billy found a good knife in the utensil drawer and started gutting the fish. "Supposed to rain all day?" He asked his mother.

"I think so. Pretty heavy, too. Your father walked to work this mornin'. If it stays like this, Uncle Dave said he'd go and pick him up after work."

"Where is Uncle Dave?"

"He went out to see about finding some work. Didn't hear about any, just figured he'd let people know he was lookin'."

"Timmy's dad just went to work over at the woolen mill in Wilton," Billy remarked. Timmy Cutler was Billy's best friend who lived at the bottom of the hill by the tracks. They had met in school, three years ago, when Billie moved to the 'Hill'.

"That's wonderful," Sophie replied. "I'll tell Uncle Dave when he gets back. Maybe he could check over there."

Billy finished cleaning the fish and grabbed a small pot from one of the cupboards. He carefully washed each fish and dropped them into the pot. They would stay nice and cool in the refrigerator until his mother got them ready for supper. He finished cleaning up the mess of fish heads and guts, grabbed the stick and threw everything out into the trash can in the shed. Sophie had fixed them some soup and sandwiches while he was cleaning the fish. She called Jake down and the boys had a quick lunch. The rain continued for the entire afternoon and the boys resigned themselves to a boring day indoors. Billy spent most of the afternoon reading a new Hardy Boys mystery in his room.

Dave returned in late afternoon and was busy patching some holes in the shed that the raccoons had dug through to get after the garbage. Jake had heard Dave's pickup drive into the yard. He headed downstairs to help Dave in the shed. Billy joined them around five o'clock.

"I heard you boys got caught in the rain today," Dave said, grinning and pointing to the clothes that were hanging along the wall.

"Yeah, we got caught right in the middle of the thunder and lightnin'. Didn't bother me none, but Jake was scared."

"Was not!" Jake yelled back as he pushed Billy on the arm. He certainly didn't want Uncle Dave to think he was scared. After all, he was 11, and a young man.

"Sure looked like it to me," Billy snickered. "You ran for that shed like a jackrabbit. I could barely keep up."

"Just didn't want to get wet, that's all," Jake mumbled as he looked down and kicked the floor of the shed.

Dave could see that Jake was unhappy with the conversation. "Well, that makes sense. Guess I would have done the same thing." Jake's expression lightened, happy to hear Uncle Dave agree with him.

"Well, I gotta finish this up. I'm supposed to pick your father up around six thirty. Don't need him walking home in the pouring rain."

"Okay. Hey Jake, let's go out to the barn for a while." Billy started running through the sheds making the sound of a cackling chicken.

Jake took off after him yelling, "CUT IT OUT!"

The sheds attached to the left front side of the barn with the door leading into the barn. The barn itself was old and worn, but still in pretty good shape. There were two large sliding doors centered in the front with rusty pulley wheels that rolled along and equally rusty track. The track was attached to the barn over the doors on the outside. The wheels would make a horrific screeching noise as you pushed the doors apart. Looking back into the barn, the center was wide and open, all the way to the back wall. On the right were three horse stalls, followed by three boxed in pens, each with a half wall in the front. The pens were probably used in the past for beef cows or goats, maybe even some sheep. The door that led to the sheds was on the left. There were two large boxed pens on the left, which also had the half walls. The first one had chicken wire covering the front from the half wall up to the loft floor. The second one was obviously used for pigs, as the old trough was still visible against the back wall. Above the stalls and pens, on both sides, were the hay lofts.

Looking above the lofts, the massive wooden beams crisscrossed as they worked their way to the peak. The beams were covered with barn swallow nests everywhere you look. Most of the hay stored in the lofts last year was gone. Things would soon change when the August hay was cut, and bailed. The first cut in June usually went into the barns at the dairy.

Once they were filled, the rest would be brought down and stored in this barn for backup during the winter.

The boys darted through the sheds, into the barn and headed down past the chicken wire. A wooden ladder, attached to the wall boards between the two pens, led up to the loft. There were several beams they could walk across to get from one loft to the other. Sometimes they would pretend they were circus performers and walk across the beams as if they were on tightropes. They would wobble side to side, pretending they were losing their balance and trying not to fall.

A long brown braided rope hung from one of the high beams over the left loft. They could stand on the bales of hay at one end of the loft, swing out on the rope and land on the bales at the other end of the loft. They called it their Tarzan swing. The barn was a great place to play, especially when the weather was bad.

"Ain't been out here in a while." Billy said as he headed up the ladder. Jake was right behind him. Billy sat down and laid his head back and looked up towards the top of the barn. "Look, Jake, there's babies in some of them nests."

The barn swallow was a beautiful bird. It was blue-black on top from its head to its tail. Its underbelly was a cinnamon color with a dark orange-brown throat. It had a true swallow-tail, deeply forked, in the shape of a "V" with white tail spots. "They sure are noisy," Jake commented as they lay there watching the birds swooping in and out of the barn. You could hear the babies chirping as the parents brought them their food. The boys lost track of time as they played and swung on the Tarzan swing. It seemed like they had just gotten there, when they heard Uncle Dave's voice.

"Hey, you two. Your mother wants you in the house to get ready for supper. I'm going to pick up your dad. Be back in a few minutes."

The boys descended from the loft and headed back through the sheds and into the house. Dave made a mad dash through the rain and into his truck, backed out of the drive, and headed out to pick up Josh.

When Josh and Dave came into the house, the boys were on the couch and Sophie was in the kitchen. She looked exceptionally lovely this evening. Her hair was combed out down to her shoulders and she was wearing one of her newer summer dresses. "Ain't fit fa man nor beast out there!" Josh bellowed as he shook the rain from his head and wiped his hands down his pants. He took off his plastic rain jacket and hung it on the rack by the door. "Good thing I had this taday. Rain should be done by mornin', so they say." He never did put too much trust the weather man.

"You boys catch me some trout taday, did ya?"

"They ain't just for you, dad. We got enough for all of us," Jake piped in.

"Well, ya know I kin eat a dozen or so myself," Josh said laughingly. He walked to the kitchen, came up behind Sophie, and put his arms around her waist. He gently kissed her cheek and said, "you're lookin' mighty fine this evenin' Mrs. Baka."

She felt a flush come to her cheeks and she wondered if he had remembered about today. "Now Josh Baker, what's gotten into you? Better get washed up for supper, everything's ready."

He let go of her waist and waltzed over to the sink, humming Hank Williams, "Lovesick Blues", as he went. Sophie had pan-fried the trout just the way the boys liked them. They were rolled in flour and fried in about an inch of butter. She served them up on a platter along with some vegetables, baked potatoes and salad greens. "That was delicious as usual," Dave said as he finished up, leaned back in his chair and began to pat his stomach. Everyone else finished up and Sophie started to get up from the table to clean up.

"DON'T NO ONE LEAVE THA TABLE!" Josh said in a strong and demanding voice. "I got some serious business ta talk about!" Sophie looks surprised as she sat back down in her chair. The boys looked at each other as if to say, "What did you do now?"

"What's wrong, Josh?" Sophie asked in a very quiet voice.

"Well, you see – – –." He stopped his sentence and stood up. His face was stern and showed little expression. "Wait right hea. I gotta git sump-n'." The tone of his voice was still strong. He walked over to his rain jacket, reached into the pocket and pulled out a small velvet blue box. He walked back to the table and proceeded right over next to Sophie. "Hope ya like it, Mrs. Baka, Happy Anniversary!" He bent down and kissed her softly on the lips. She stood up, threw her arms around his neck and kissed him back.

"Oh, Josh, Happy Anniversary! I didn't know if you remembered it or not." Her eyes began to fill with tears. She looked down at the small box on the table. "What did you go and do now?"

"Ain't nothin'," he said as he wiped the water from her eyes with his thumbs. Sophie turned, and picked up the box. Her hands were trembling as she opened the top. She gasped and put her hand to her chest as if to catch her breath. "Oh my Lord!" Now the tears were flowing down her cheeks.

Inside the box was a beautiful silver and gold cross pendant necklace. Along the top of the cross were four birthstones representing Josh, her, and the two boys. She had seen it months ago at a store over in Farmington and had mentioned to him how beautiful it was.

"I just can't believe it, how, when?"

"Ordered it a while back. Had Dave pick it up earlier taday. Ya like it, huh?"

"I love it!" She exclaimed. She slid the pendant from the box, the long neck chain sliding out from the bottom, put the chain around her neck and fastened it in the back. She couldn't stop staring at the cross. It was so beautiful and had so much meaning. The boys, in the meantime, had breathed a sigh of relief realizing that they weren't in any trouble – this time.

"Happy anniversary, dad. Happy anniversary, mom," they both chipped in. Dave followed with congratulations of his own. It had gotten silent so Josh said, "June twenty third, nineteen fotty four, fourteen years en still goin'." He chuckled. "We best finish up hea. Long day tomorra'." Everyone help with cleanup and the boys were ready to head up to bed.

"Billy," Sophie said. "You and Jake's knives are on top of the radio. Some piece of paper to, with scribbling on it. You left them in your pants in the shed."

THE PAPER! He had forgotten all about it when they changed their wet clothes. "Thanks, mom." He walked over to the radio and picked up their knives and the piece of paper. He headed upstairs thinking he had better be more careful with the paper from now on.

Mr. Fitzpatrick's Day

Today was Thursday, the Fourth of July. The summer was skipping by at a rapid pace. It was bright and clear, and approaching eighty degrees. It was a day the 'Hill' looked forward to every year. If they all had their way, it would be called Mr. Fitzpatrick's day. Every house on the hill was busy preparing for the evening festivities. It had become a yearly ritual that everyone brought some food, drink, and other goodies to share with everyone else. They would set everything out on the big tables that Mr. Fitzpatrick sets up in his backyard. Most everyone would show up around 8:00 pm to start eating and conversing.

By mid-afternoon, Sophie had finished getting her contributions ready for the nightime celebration. She had made fresh-baked apple pie, fried chicken pieces, potato salad and two jugs of fresh squeezed lemonade.

The boys were out behind the barn helping Dave weed the vegetable garden. It had been planted with everything that Sophie had asked for this year. It was about 40 feet long and 10 to 12 rows wide. Their father had put chicken wire around the entire garden to keep the animals out. The corn had been planted in the top corner followed by some tomato plants Sophie had started in the house in some egg cartons. There were carrots, beets, string beans, squash, pumpkins and cukes. There was a small area for radishes and for the first time, several potato plants. It was fair to say that the entire garden was completely occupied. "You guys excited about tonight?" Dave asked in a loud voice.

"Can't wait," said Billy. "It's always a fun time."

"Wait till you see it!" Jake yelled from the end of the garden. "All kinds of colors and it gets pretty loud sometimes!"

"Oh, I know," Dave said. "I've seen them before." They continued on with their weeding activities until several minutes later, when Billie stopped sat back on his sneakers.

"Uncle Dave! You believe in buried treasure and stuff like that?"

Jake had moved closer by this time and heard Billy asked the question. He looked over at him, thinking that Billy was about to tell their uncle about the paper.

"Well, that all depends," Dave replied. He stopped raking and rested his arms across the top of the handle. How come you're asking?"

"Just wondering, that's all," was the response.

The story that George had told him at the store popped into Dave's mind. "Could be that there's buried treasure right around here. Especially with all those bank robberies that took place."

"Bank robberies!" Billy exclaimed. Jake heard it to and came up closer to Dave.

"That's what I said," Dave replied. "You two listen up and I'll tell you what happened." The boys were too young to remember anything about the robberies that happened eleven years ago. They both moved in closer and sat down. Dave began to tell them what had happened when they were just little ones. He enhanced certain parts of the story as he went along, to make it more exciting. The boys stared at him, mouths open and eyes bugged. They were getting more and more infatuated the deeper he got into the story. A voice broke in from the edge of the barn. It was Sophie carrying a tray that held three large glasses of lemonade.

"Figured with the heat, you boys could use a nice cold drink. Don't need you shrivelin' up to nothin' out here in the sun."

"Thanks, Soph," Dave said smiling. He noticed Sophie looking at the boys sitting on the ground. "Soph," he said as she was passing out the drinks. "I was just telling the boys about those bank robberies a while back, hope that's okay?"

Her mouth curled up and she shook her head. "If they get nightmares from it, it'll be your fault, David Clough. Just a bunch of nonsense, that's what it is. You boys don't pay it no mind."

Dave laughed and looked over at Billy and Jake. "They'll be just fine, won't you boys?" They both shook their heads in agreement. Sophie headed back to the house still shaking her head as she left. She disappeared around the corner of the barn. Dave finished up with the final details of the story. "Guess they never did find all that stolen money. Who knows, maybe they hid it right here on the farm."

"Anyone ever know who they were?" Billy asked.

"Oh, yeah. Their names were Sam Green and Frank Walker. They lived right around here and both of them used to work for the dairy, years back."

"WOW!" Jake shouted. "That's really neat. Maybe that's got something to do---." He stopped his sentence as Billy looked over at him and gave him a quick scowl. Billy's stomach was in a knot. There was a lump forming in his throat and his heart was racing a mile a minute. He pictured the paper in his mind and felt that there was some kind of connection with what his uncle had just told them. He needed to look at it as soon as possible. His mind was wandering off in all directions.

"Billy, hey Billy!" Dave was pushing him on the shoulder. Billy jerked back and looked up at Dave. "Quite a look on your face," Dave said, grinning. "You okay?"

"Sure," Billy answered quickly. "I was just thinking about them robbers."

"Oh, it's just a story, – true though," Dave replied back. "We better get this garden finished before the sun cooks us out here." The sun had gotten stronger as the afternoon wore on. They finished their weeding, picked up the rakes and hoes and headed back toward the house. Billy's mind was still wandering.

"We'll put the tools in the shed," he said to Dave as they came around the front of the barn. "Tell mom we'll be in the barn playin'."

"Sure," said Dave as he headed for the front door.

The boys dropped the tools in the second shed. "Come on!" Billy said with excitement in his voice as he raced for the barn. "We gotta check something out!" Jake was right on his heels as they headed up into the loft. Billy jumped up on a bale of hay and then sat on the one behind it. Jake followed and sat beside him. Billy reached into his pocket and pulled out the paper. He laid it out flat and looked down at the writing. His heart started pounding again. It was right there in front of him – SG 35   FW 35   TINY 30.

"Look!" He hit Jake with his elbow. "SG, it stands for Sam Green and FW must be Frank Walker. It's right here on the paper." He could hardly contain his excitement. Jake was starting to become interested once again.

"What do you think it means, Billy?" Jake asked.

"Don't know yet, but them initials sure match up. It's gotta have something to do with them robberies, it's gotta!"

"How about TINY, what's that."

Billy shook his head. "Guess it could be someone else. Uncle Dave said there was talk about a third person, remember?" Jake nodded as Billy continued. "Wish I knew what this other stuff was, especially the last line. ST-2 Left Side. Just don't make any sense to me. I'm gonna tell Timmy tonight at the fireworks. Maybe he can help us figure it out."

"He's gonna blab it all over," Jake said as he gave Billy a look of disgust.

"No, he won't," Billy replied. "I'll tell him that we're keeping it a secret. Come on. Let's get back to the house." He stuffed the paper back into his pocket and they headed for the sheds, zipped through, and entered the house. The radio was on low and Dave and Sophie were sitting, conversing about the garden. She looked over as they came in.

"Oh, there you are. You too need to get cleaned up. Dad's gonna' be home pretty quick. He's doing an early milkin' so he'll have time to get home and ready for tonight. Change your clothes and put on something clean."

"Okay, mom," came the replies. The boys proceeded on to the upstairs bathroom to get ready.

It was just past 8 pm and time to go. Everyone was ready and excited. The boys were up in their room talking about the robberies and coming up with all kinds of possible solutions for the paper and places where the money could be. Josh's voice bellowed up the stairs. "Okay you two, let's go!"

Sophie had everything they were taking sitting out on the table. As the boys came bounding down the stairs, she pointed to the table and spouted, "Everyone grab something. I'll get the blankets." With food, drinks and blankets in hand, they headed out the door and down the drive. Most everyone walked to the event, but there were already several cars lined up on the roadside near Mr. Fitzpatrick's house.

The event seemed to draw more and more people every year as the word spread around the area. They walked up the driveway and entered the backyard through the arched breezeway between the garage and the house. There were several long tables set up near the back of the house. They were already filled with a variety of food and drink. About 15 to 20 people had already set up their blankets and chairs. Mr. Fitzpatrick was talking to a man over near the tables. He saw them come into the yard and headed towards them.

"Sophie, Josh, how's everyone doing?" He seemed in great spirits this particular evening. "Hi boys, and who is this gentleman with you?"

"This is my brother David, Ed," Sophie said. "He's stayin' with us for a while."

"Pleased to meet you," he said quickly to Dave. "Now put your stuff over on the tables and pick yourself a nice piece of lawn. Should be a good group. Seems to be more every year. Fireworks will start at ten sharp. You know I spent all afternoon setting them up." More people were filing in through the breezeway. "Gotta go," Ed said as he headed to greet them.

"Okay, Ed," Josh said.

"Nice meeting you," Dave remarked as he started walking towards the tables. Billy had just sat the pot of potato salad on the table when he heard Timmy's voice.

"Hey, Billy!" Timmy yelled.

"Hi, Timmy. Where you guys sitting?"

"Mom and my sisters are right over there." He pointed to a blanket towards the back of the lawn. "Dad's coming up in a few."

Jake walked up to the table and stood next to Billy. "Hi, Timmy," he said.

"Hi, Jake." The three of them headed back towards where Timmy's mom and sisters were sitting.

Josh, Sophie, and Dave found a piece of lawn off to the right and spread the blankets out on the ground. Once they had everything settled, Sophie led Dave all around the yard. She introduced him to everyone she knew and met some new people along the way. Sophie loved to socialize, although she didn't get much chance to.

Everett Robinson had arrived with Fred and Skip from the dairy. He probably wouldn't stay for the fireworks, but he always made an appearance. His brother, Carl, never came out much. He spent most of his time cooped up in the house at the dairy. Josh had told the family that he had heard that Carl had some type of a sugar disease and only had a few months left to live.

Everyone was mingling in and out across the yard. David struck up a conversation with the man that Mr.

Fitzpatrick had been talking to when they first arrived. Sophie was flittering around the yard, catching up on all the latest "talk" of the town. Josh had gone over and was talking to Fred, Skip, and Mr. Robinson. Mr. Robinson left shortly after to head back to the dairy. The sun had snuggled down behind Spruce Mountain and the pink and blue hues of the evening sunset swept across the horizon. The temperature was still in the 70s. It was a perfect evening for the event.

Billy, Jake, and Timmy had gathered off to the right side of the yard. The fireflies had come out and there were hundreds of them blinking their signals out over the fields surrounding the house and the yard. Some of the kids were running along the edge of the field trying to catch a few of the close ones. Somewhere between late afternoon and now, Billy had decided not to tell Timmy about the paper. He figured he would wait until a later time. They stood there talking about an upcoming fishing trip and things they had been doing this summer. Everyone wandered back and forth to the tables helping themselves to a multitude of food and drink. The boys had made several trips, loading up their plates, trying to sample everything.

Out of nowhere came a flash of light followed by a loud explosion that rang everyone's eardrums. Someone on a blanket near the front let out a scream. Mr. Fitzpatrick had lit a cherry bomb behind the garage. It had scared everyone half to death. "IT'S TIME!" He yelled, laughing as he started walking toward the roped off area along the back of the yard.

He signaled to the man up at the tables and a few seconds later the two floodlights that had brightened up the darkness in the backyard, went out. He had spent all afternoon digging small round holes, 6 to 8 inches deep, and placed a large soup can down each one. He then placed one of the fireworks rockets in each can so that everything was ready for his display. There were about 100 in total. It would take him about 45 minutes to light them all off. He started with the first can, lighting a match and sticking it down into the can to light the fuse. As quick as he lit it, he jumped away from the area.

WOOSH!!! It was the sound of the rocket shooting up out of the can and into the night sky. In a few seconds the sky lit up with a brilliant display of blue, white, and red streaks thrown out in all directions. You could hear the ooh's and ah's echo across the lawn. He continued down the line following the same procedure each time. As each rocket exploded it filled the sky with its own unique array of colors and shapes until they've faded and disappeared into the darkness. Every so often he would light off a cherry bomb or a string of firecrackers to keep everyone awake and on their toes.

When he finally reached the last one, he yelled to the group, "Last One, folks!" Before he lit the final fuse, he set off a string of firecrackers that he had connected together and stretched out about 10 feet. They snap and pop as they exploded down the line. He lit the final fuse, and the last rocket, with a red white and blue display similar to the very first, exploded and faded quickly into the night sky. Everyone was yelling and applauding.

"What a great show!"

"Nice job, Mr. Fitzpatrick!"

"Thank you so much. Can't wait till next year!"

Comments were being yelled in from all over the lawn. "Thank you, thank you all for coming!" Ed yelled back. You could tell that this was something that he really enjoyed doing every year. He waved his hand up towards the house and the two floodlights shot back on and lit up the backyard. He then walked up and stood by the breezeway while everyone gathered their blankets and grabbed their pots and dishes from the tables. As they filed out, he thanked each one for coming.

"Ed, that was terrific," Josh said. "Thanks."

" Yes it was so wonderful," Sophie joined in.

"Sure was," the boys added.

Dave extended his hand. "It was nice to meet you – what a great job!"

"Thank you, thank you," Ed replied.

They headed through the breezeway and down the driveway, yelling goodbyes to a multitude of people heading in all directions. It only took a few minutes to get home. As they entered the house, Sophie said, "What a wonderful time. He does such a great job every year. It's just hard to believe. You boys better get up to bed now, it's almost eleven thirty." Billy and Jake headed upstairs as Dave plopped down on the couch, leaned back, stretched his arms up and out, and performed a silent yawn. He dropped his hands into his lap and looked over at Josh who had just settled down in his chair.

"Remember that man that was standing around near the tables? You know, the one Ed was talking to when we first got there."

"Yup, remember seein' em," Josh replied. "Never did get a chance ta meet em. I think I saw em there last year too."

"Well, I talked with him for a while. You'll never guess who he is."

Josh shrugged his shoulders and Sophie looked over inquisitively at Dave.

"He was the cop that Mr. Fitzpatrick patched up during that shoot out with those robbers. How about that!"

"Well I'll be," Sophie explained. "That is something."

"Don't that seem kinda strange?" Josh asked.

"I guess," Dave answered, shrugging his shoulders. "The way he told me, they had gotten together after it happened and they've been friends ever since. Funny how things come around in this world"

"Sure is," Josh said.

It'd been a long exciting day and the boys were tired. Josh and Sophie said their good nights on their way to bed. Jake fell right off to sleep. Billy laid there mumbling to himself about the paper and the lettering on it. "There's gotta be more clues. What does all the other stuff mean? Maybe there's more clues in the cellar." His thoughts led him into a deep sleep.

The following week shot by faster than one could blink and nothing had really happened during that time. Billy and Jake had been able to get down to the cellar on several occasions. They checked all the cracks and rocks, but found nothing to help them unravel their mystery paper.

It was now Friday, the 12th of July, just a bit past noon. Josh had just finished his lunch and returned to the dairy. Sophie was hanging out a load of clothes and Dave had left to go to Wilton, still looking for work. Billy hopped off the stump near the clothesline and headed for the barn. Jake was already in the barn playing when Billy walked in. Where are you, Jake?" Billy yelled.

"Up here," came the voice from the loft. Billy climbed up the ladder the loft, just as Jake was swinging by on the rope. "AH A AH A AH A AH A AH" Jake belted out, trying to imitate the Tarzan yell. He landed on the bales of hay, jumped down and came over towards Billy. "Want to play hide and seek?" He asked.

"Yeah, I guess so," replied Billy. "Nothin' else to do."

Jake knelt down next to a bale of hay and said, "You hide first." He put his head down hay bale with his hands alongside, and started counting slowly to twenty-five. Billy took off down the ladder and into the first old horse stall across the barn. There were some old crates in the corner and he snuggled down behind them to keep out of sight. He could still hear Jake counting. "Twenty-one, twenty-two, twenty-three, twenty-four, twenty-five. Here I come, ready or not."

He could hear Jake's footsteps right above him. Jake had crossed over and was checking the other loft. Some pieces of hay and dust were falling through the cracks and down into the stall. The footsteps went away. Jake cross the beam and headed for the ladder. He climbed down and walked up and down the barn, peeking into each of the boxed areas and the horse stalls.

He finally got to the first stall, leaned against the half wall and peered in. Billy was still crunched down behind the crates trying to breathe as quietly as possible so that Jake would not hear him. Apparently, Billy wasn't down quite far enough because Jake could see the very top of Billy's hair sticking out over the top of the crates.

"Got ya!" Jake yelled, pointing to the corner. "Right there behind them crates. Come on out. My turn to hide." As he started to back away from the half wall, his belt buckle caught the edge of a piece of thin wood attached to the wall. It loosened and fell to the barn floor. Billy came out through the swinging door just as Jake was bending down to pick it up.

"What's that?" Billy asked.

"Don't know, it just fell off the wall." Jake was pointing to where he had been standing. "Musta been loose. Caught the edge of my buckle on it." Jake held the piece of wood up, and brushed it off. It was about 4 inches wide and 6 inches long. "There's something on it," Jake said to Billy as he handed it across.

It appeared that someone had burnt some letters and numbers into the wood, but they had faded over time. Billy took it and rubbed his fingers across the wood. He could feel the indentation as his fingers slid across. He wet his finger and started over again, tracing the indents as he went. He spoke very slowly as he traced each one. "S - - - - - T - - - - -Dash - - - - One." Then he repeated it quicker. "S T Dash One." He stopped and thought for a minute, remembering something about the dairy barn when they were doing the milking. Each stall for the cows is labeled with a tag so that his dad could identify which stall the milk had come from when they were checking certain cows.

"Could be some kind of marker for the stall," he said as he looked down the wall to the other stalls. "Look, there's one there too." He pointed to the second stall. He walked over and traced his finger over the piece of wood on the second stall. "This one is ST Dash Two."

Jake had gone down to the third stall. "Number three on this one," Jake answered back.

When Jake looked over, Billy's face looked like he had seen a ghost. His hands were shaking as he fumbled with his pocket. "It can't be!" he said nervously, as he pulled the crumpled paper from his pocket. "ST dash Two, remember Jake, it's on the paper!" He could hardly spit out the words.

Billy smoothed out the paper against his knee and held it up. "Look! Right here!" He pointed to the bottom line. ST-2 LEFT SIDE glared back at them, plain as day. Billy grabbed the door to the second stall, swung it open, and darted inside. Jake was right behind him.

"What are we doing?" Jake asked.

"What do you mean?" Billy replied. "We gotta check it out. Could be anything. Maybe they hid the money in here. Just look around."

"Left side, left side," Billy kept repeating as he walked over to that side of the stall. There was only half-light inside the stall because of its enclosures, but it was bright enough to see just about everything. There was a rusty mouth bit hanging on a nail with several frayed straps of leather dangling down along the wall. The floor had about an inch or more of hay and dust that had accumulated from dropping through the cracks of the loft floor above.

Jake was checking out a couple of empty boxes in the corner while Billy began feeling up and down each board on the wall to see if anything looked or felt out of place. "Please, there's gotta be something here, anything," he mumbled to himself as he moved along the wall. He reached the corner with no results. There appeared to be nothing out of place, there were just plain old barn boards with a few nails sticking out. "Hey Jake, bring them boxes over here."

"What for?" Jake questioned.

"I want to check up by the beams," Billy said as he pointed to the top edge of the stall. He tipped the first box upside down and pushed it up tight against the wall. Then he placed the second box on top of the first, in the same manner. "Hold them tight while I climb up," he said to Jake. "And keep an eye out for mom, in case she's lookin' for us."

Jake backed up into the boxes and pushed with his backside to keep them pressed against the wall. This way he could steady the boxes and still see if his mother was coming into the barn. Billy climbed up onto the boxes and got into a kneeling position. He slowly stood up, using the wall as a balancing point. With his arm fully stretched, his hand could reach the small opening between the top of the beam and the loft floor. He started in the corner to his right and worked his hand back towards him. He turned his body against the wall with his arm directly overhead. Then he switched arms and continued checking down the beam to his left. His hand was about two feet down the beam to the left when his fingers hit against something stringy. His hand stopped.

"I can feel something. Can't tell what it is."

Jake leaned his head way back, and looked up at Billy. "Can you get it?"

"I'm tryin' to get hold of it," Billy responded.

He grasped as much of the stringy material that he could and began to pull. It wouldn't move. He pushed himself up on his toes to try to grasp a bigger handful of the material. He was pulling as hard as he could, still nothing. Suddenly, it broke loose and Billy's body lurched backwards off the boxes.

"LOOK OUT!" Billy cried out to Jake.

Jake turned, and jumped out of the way as the top box when flying towards the corner of the stall. Billy landed flat out on his back with a loud thud.

Jake rushed over to his side. "Billy, you okay?"

"I think so," Billy said, looking a little dazed. His left hand was still clutching the material that he had pulled out from the beam. His right forearm had about an eight inch string of blood starting just below the elbow. He had scraped his arm on a rusty nail sticking out of the boards on the wall.

"Hey, ya bleedin!" Jake said, pointing to Billy's arm.

"Knew I felt something when I lost my balance." He let go of the material, pushed himself up on his knees, and looked at his arm. "Just a little scratch. Stings a bit, that's all."

"What is it? What did you find?" Jake's voice sounded excited.

The material lay in front of them on the floor. It appeared to be a folded up burlap bag. Billy reached down and picked it up. He shook it gently and said, "It's got something wrapped up in it." He set it back down and began to unfold the bag. Once unfolded, it exposed a small, dark brown wooden cigar box. There was a faded golden label on the top that read, GARCIA-HAVANA". They were both bug-eyed as Billy slowly opened the cover. Their excitement faded and their stares turned to disappointment as they looked in. NO MONEY! Once again, their hopes of buried treasure and bank loot had been crushed. There was however, something in the box. It was a large piece of paper, much bigger than the first one, folded in half and lying flat on the bottom of the box.

"Let's get it up to the loft," Billy said. He tossed the old burlap bag in the corner behind the boxes. They headed out the door of the stall, crossed over to the ladder, and climbed up into the loft. As Billy tipped the cigar box upside down, the top swung open and the paper fluttered its way to the loft floor.

"Just more stupid paper," Jake muttered. Billy picked it up, unfolded it, and laid it lengthwise on a bale of hay. The paper showed some weathering but was in good condition.

"Oh, great," Billy said in a disgruntled voice. He stared at the letters SM in the top left corner of the paper. There was a semi-circle that started near the left edge, about halfway down the paper. It looped up to the middle of the top edge and then back down to the right edge. Under the semi-circle, a crooked row of little dash marks made their way across the full length of the paper. About 2 inches down from the top left of the semicircle was a small one inch square box. There were five short lines straight up and down along the top edge of the box, with three other lines bunched together on the upper left side of the box. On the right side of the semicircle, there was an "N" with an arrow next to it that, pointing to the top of the paper. Next to that was "3TR". Underneath all this it said, "100 FT".

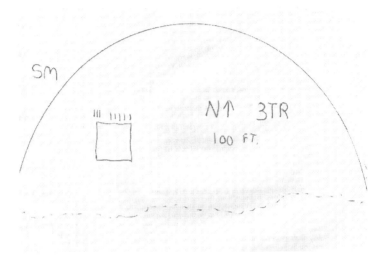

"It's gotta be a map or something," Billy said, shaking his head, while staring at the paper. "Maybe they hid the money somewhere and didn't want anyone to know."

"You think so?" Jake asked as his eyes widened.

"Don't know. Don't know nothin' and we can't tell nothin' from this," he said in a frustrated tone.

They heard the engine of Dave's pickup truck as it pulled up into the gravel drive. "Uncle Dave's back!" Jake said quickly. "We gotta hide this stuff." Billy folded the paper quickly and laid it back into the cigar box. His head darted side to side looking for a good place to hide their latest discovery. He walked along the edge of the loft to the front of the barn. He stuffed the cigar box behind the hay bales that were piled along the wall. These would be the last bales to be taken should someone come to get more hay for the dairy. The box would be safe and out of sight there. He returned to the front of the loft and he and Jake made their way down the ladder. They headed out of the barn and into the gravel drive. Dave was over by the clothes line talking to Sophie, who was working on her third basket of laundry, as the boys walked toward them.

As the boys approached, Dave yelled out, "What are you two up to?"

"Nothin'," Jake said in a slightly defensive voice. "Right Billy?"

"Yeah, just playin' in the barn," Billy replied as he gave Jake a quick stare.

It was just then that Sophie looked over and caught sight of Billy's arm. The blood from his scratch had spread and dried down his arm making it look much worse than it was. "BILLY!" She shrieked. "What happened to your arm?" She came running out from between the clothes lines and grabbed his wrist. She lifted his arm up in the air to get a better look.

"It's just a scratch, mom. I caught it on a nail in the barn."

"Get right into the house and wash it! Right now! We'll get some iodine on it. Don't want it to get infected. Let's go!"

"Aw, mom," Billy whined.

"William, GIT!" She said pointing to the front door. He knew that tone in her voice. She had called him William! There was nothing else that could be said. He headed to the house as Sophie followed him, shaking her head and mumbling. Billy walked into the kitchen and went over to the sink. Sophie tossed him a wet wash cloth and he proceeded to wipe up and down his arm to remove the dried blood. "Use some soap," Sophie said as she reached up into one of the cupboards and took out the iodine. "Gotta' kill them germs."

Billy grabbed the bar of soap at the back of the sink and scrubbed it up and down on his arm. When the soap covered the scratch, his face winced a bit from the stinging sensation that it gave him. Sophie motioned for him to come over by the cupboard.

"Dry it up and get over here."

He held his arm up and she applied the iodine to the area. "Ain't as bad as it looked," she said smiling at Billy. "Make sure you put some salve on it before you go to bed tonight."

"Okay mom, thanks." Billy looked at his arm and could see that the iodine had colored the skin around the scratch a deep yellow-orange. It actually looked worse than the scratch itself. He headed back outside and Sophie followed to finish hanging the clothes. As they left the house, Dave was walking towards them with the empty clothes basket in his hand. "Jake and I finished hanging them up for you," he said to Sophie.

She took the basket from his hands. "Well, thanks to both of you, that was really nice," she said, and with a courteous nod of her head, she turned and walked back into the house. The boys were hungry and headed into the house after her to get some lunch. After a quick lunch, they spent the rest of the afternoon helping Dave cut and rake the lawns.

That evening as they sat down to supper, Josh looked across at Billy's arm and motioned towards it with his head. "What happened to ya?"

Billy held his arm up. "Just a scratch, that's all. Mom put some iodine on it. Just made it look worse."

"Well, good thing it ain't no worse. I need ya ta help me out at tha dairy."

"When?"

"Startin' tomorra'," Josh answered. "Skips gotta go home for a bit. Seems his dad is sick en they don't know if he's gonna' make it. Probably be gone for a week or so." Billy's face saddened. A week or so! He had been planning to work at solving the paper mystery. Now, he'd have to wait until later. "Hate ta interrupt ya fun, but I do need ya help."

"That's okay, dad, hope Skip's dad will be okay." Billy said. "I was getting bored anyway." Josh looked over knowing it was a lie, but he just smiled at Billy and shook his head in agreement.

Josh, Dave, and Sophie talked about the situation at the dairy throughout the rest of supper. Before you knew it, bedtime had arrived, the boys said their good nights, and headed upstairs. They were talking about the newly discovered paper as they climbed into bed. The salve on his arm had Billy moving around carefully under the covers. He was trying to lay his arm down without wiping all the salve off. He looked over at Jake, and said, "Don't bother the box in the barn until we can get it together." Jake agreed. They both fell asleep, thinking about the new drawings and what clues it could hold.

Cowboys and Indians

Billy helped his father out at the dairy, and the days skipped by. On July 25, Skip returned to work and Billy found out that Skip's father had passed away the prior week and had been buried over the weekend. "Life's unfair sometimes," Josh told Billy. "Ya just don't know what it'll bring. Gotta be prepared for anything." Billy, at the age of thirteen, could never imagine what it would be like if something ever happened to his mom or dad.

A lot of things had happened in the last week and a half. A friend of Josh's had dropped off a couple of cords of wood next to the sheds. Dave had been cutting, splitting, and storing it in the shed. Jake came down with the chickenpox and was confined to his room for the past week. Sophie finally decided that his contagious days had passed and he could get out of his room. Billy had been sleeping on a cot in with Uncle Dave. He would be able to move back in with Jake now that the chickenpox had dried up and were just about gone.

Billy and his dad had been using some time to get a few things ready for the Farmington Fair that was coming up the first week of August. Every year, the dairy would take some of its newest equipment and put on display, along with two or three of their best milkers for judging. This year Josh would be at the fair demonstrating the equipment and tending to the cows. Everett Robinson had submitted Josh's name for the "Dairyman of the Year" award. The award was given out each year to the best dairyman in the area.

Sophie had been quite busy, also. Every year she would make a quilt that would be auctioned off to benefit the Farmington children's orphanage. The quilt was almost complete, except for a few finishing touches that she would see to over the next week.

Dave had been the busiest of all. If you headed up through the field towards the dairy, there was a rocky area that humped up right out of the ground, just like a whales back. It was about 500 feet up from the house. There was one big tree that had grown right up in the middle of the hump. Dave had taken some time over the past weekend and built a tree house platform in amongst the lower branches. He had installed a rope ladder that attached to one of the big branches which led right up to the platform. Once the boys climbed up, they would be able to pull the rope ladder up to keep everyone else out. He hadn't told the boys about it yet. He had been waiting for Jake to recuperate from his ailment. That way he could surprise them together.

Josh had already left for work that morning and Dave and the boys were having breakfast with Sophie. Jake was sitting there, his face covered with tiny red spots, the final remnants of his fleeing chickenpox. Dave and Billy were both staring at his face.

"Looks like you had a fight with dad's ice pick," Billy said jokingly.

"Billy! Don't be picking on your brother," Sophie piped in. "Them spots will all disappear in a couple of days," she said quickly looking at Jake. "You won't even know they were there."

When they finished breakfast, Dave said, "I need you boys to help me out this morning."

"Doing what," Billy asked, quickly. He had hoped that he and Jake could get out to the barn they hadn't been able to look at the paper in the box for the last two weeks.

Oh, just a special project, you'll see," Dave replied. He looked at Sophie and smiled. He had told her about the treehouse a few days earlier and she knew the boys would be very excited when they saw it.

They all help clean up after breakfast and then Dave motioned to the boys. "Let's go! Can't be hanging around in here all day." He headed out the door with the boys right on his heels. He crossed the gravel drive, past the old stump, and kept walking right past the clotheslines.

As they reached the edge of the field, Jake blurted out, "Where we going?"

Dave started up through the field. "Just up there by that old tree," Dave said as he pointed towards the hump up in the field.

"Ain't nothin' up there but a bunch of rocks," Billy thought to himself. "Why we goin' up there?"

They soon approached the rocky mound and the boys could see something hanging down alongside the tree.

"What's that?" Jake asked.

Dave walked up over the rocks stood at the base of the tree. He looked at the boys and then pointed up towards the branches. "It takes you right up there."

"WOW!" The boys shouted out in unison as they looked up to see the wide, flat platform nestled in amongst the branches of the tree.

"I figured you guys could use another place to play. That old barn must get kind of boring after a while. This can be like your own secret hideout. Come on, let's get up there. You first, Jake."

Jake started climbing the rope ladder, but seemed a little nervous as the ladder started swaying a bit from his weight. David set it up so that they could step right off the ladder and onto the platform. Jake finally made it to the top and gingerly stepped out onto the platform. Billy didn't need any invitation. He zipped up the ladder and onto the platform next to Jake. Dave followed them up and joined them at the top.

"I wanted to put sides and a top on it," Dave said to the boys. "Just didn't have enough room with all these big branches overhead."

"This is just fine," Billy answered back.

"Sure is!" Jake echoed.

"You guys can play all sorts of stuff up here. Cops and robbers, cowboys and Indians, it's all imagination. Oh, watch this!" Dave grabbed the rope ladder and started pulling it up. "You can bring the ladder right up here with you so no one can get up if you don't want them to. Then when you're ready to leave, just drop it down. So, what do you think?"

"It's really great," Billy repeated. "Thanks, Uncle Dave."

"Yeah, thanks," Jake responded.

"Great view, too." Dave pointed towards the pasture and up towards Spruce Mountain.

"See that little area up there on the mountain," Billy said as he pointed it out to Dave.

"Oh, yeah," Dave replied. "Looks like a great place to go camping."

"No way! That's the biggest and best blueberry patch in the world up there!" Billy boasted. "We get tons of them for mom every time we go. They should be ready in a few more weeks. Maybe you can go up with us sometime."

"Sure, I can do that. Sounds like fun. Thanks for asking," Dave replied.

They sat on the platform for a while talking about things the boys would be doing for the rest of the summer. They talked about fishing, camping, blueberry picking, and helping out at the dairy. "Well, boys, I gotta get back and finish some things at the house. You staying here?"

"Nah, we'll come back up later," Billy said as he looked over at Jake. "We can bring some stuff back with us." Billy had already been thinking about what a great place to bring the cigar box. They would be able to study the paper without anyone around. He started to think about how they would get it out of the barn and up to the treehouse. Dave dropped the ladder down and proceeded to climb down to the ground. Jake and Billy followed him down and they all headed back down through the field towards the house. As they passed by the clotheslines, Sophie appeared in the front doorway.

"Oh, there you are! I was just gonna' yell for you. Josh just rang up from the dairy. Some of them cows got loose from the pasture and their headed for the road. He needs you and the boys to come up and help."

"Okay!" Dave yelled as he headed towards his truck. "Jump in boys!"

Jake and Billy piled in on the passenger side. As they started to back out, Dave stuck his head out the window and yelled, "Sophie, when we get done, I gotta go down to town to get some gas. I'll take the boys with me. You need anything?"

"OK! I'm all set for now," she acknowledged, and gave them a little wave.

They backed out of the driveway, and headed to the dairy. Jake stomach was tied up in knots. He hated being around the cows when they were loose. Tied up in the barn, they were okay, but loose outside, Oh No. What was he going to do? He couldn't let anyone know that he was scared. Josh was in the driveway when they pulled into the dairy. The three of them hopped out of the truck. "Where are they?" Dave yelled.

"All ova," Josh said, waving his arms. "Fred en Skip headed out ta tha fields. Billy, you en Jake head up tha road. I think there's a couple of em crossin' that old stonewall. See if ya can shoo em back inta tha field. Me en Dave will head out this way en try ta cut off tha others."

Billy bolted towards the road. "Come on, Jake! Hurry up!"

Jake did not share the urgency of his brother, but he started running after him. As they headed up the road, they could see two of the cows had just crossed the stone wall and were milling around in the ditch next to the roadway."I'LL TAKE THE FIRST ONE!" Billy yelled. "Just get behind the other one and wave your arms and yell. Should make her go back up and over the wall."

65

Billy got behind the first cow and made sure she was headed in the right direction. He slapped her backside and then bounced back and forth, side to side, to keep her guided towards the wall. In a minute, she was up and over, and back into the field. Jake was not having as much success with his efforts. The second cow was walking further up the road while Jake remained about 10 feet away from her, waving his arms and yelling.

Billy hollered at him. "Grab her tail and pull it to the right! It'll help steer her!"

"I can do it, I can do it," Jake mumbled as he got closer to the cow reached out and grabbed her tail with both hands and pulled hard the right. She turned immediately towards the wall and with a sudden jumping motion, started running straight at it.

Billy was keeping his cow from re-crossing the wall and looked up just as Jake's cow jumped. JAKE WAS FROZEN WITH FEAR. The sudden move had knocked him off his feet, but he still had both hands grasped solidly onto the cow's tail. The cow was dragging him along the ground straight towards the stone wall! His mind was telling him to let go, but his hands wouldn't respond. They were getting closer and closer to the wall and he had his eyes shut tight. If he didn't let go, the cow would take him straight over the rocks and he could be seriously injured. Billy was running towards them as fast as he could.

Billy screen, "JAKE, LET GO! WHAT ARE YOU DOING! LET GOOOO!" He was almost there. "JAAAKE!" He screamed louder.

Jake opened his eyes as his hands loosen their grip on the cow's tail with no time to spare. The cow bolted forward and jumped over the wall, as Jake lay there crying. Billy came up and knelt down beside him.

"You okay? Wow, that was close. I thought she was gonna' take you right over the wall."

Jake set up and faced his brother. The front of his shirt had a slight tear and was covered with dirt. "Yeah, I'm okay," he said, sniffling. "It really scared me, that's all." He sniffed back his tears, wiped his eyes, and brushed off his shirt. "Don't tell dad, please! He won't ever let me help if he finds out."

"I won't," Billy said.

"Promise?" Jake blurted out.

"Yeah, I promise, Jake." Billy started to laugh. "Jake that was the damndest thing I've ever seen."

Jake's mouth was open wide as he stared at his brother. It was the first time he had ever heard his brother cuss. He started laughing along with Billy. "I won't tell dad you said that either."

"It's a deal," Billy responded still laughing. "You'd better get up. We've gotta guide these two back to the barns. Just stay off to the side. Don't let them wander to the right."

They jumped up, crossed the wall, and headed after the cows. It took about five minutes to get them to the gate near the barns. Josh, Fred, Dave, and Skip had already returned with the other escapees. As the boys approached the gate, Josh was yelling, "Good job, boys! Good job!" As the boys got closer, Josh looked over at Jake's shirt.

"That cow try ta eat ya?" Everyone started laughing.

"No, dad," Billy answered back. "He just slipped and fell in the ditch trying to get her up to the wall."

Josh put his arms around the boys' shoulders. "Well, ya both did just fine. Thanks fa tha help, Dave. I gotta git these critters inta tha barn."

"Anytime, Josh," Dave answered. "Hey, we're headed to town to gas up the truck. Already told Soph. See you at supper."

They jumped back into Dave's truck, looped around the circle drive and headed for the road. Dave turned left towards the back side of the hill. They reached the road that turned off to Beans Corner and turned right onto Woodman Hill Road.

The road was paved but it narrowed down gradually as they headed towards Old Jay Hill Road. There were a few small houses and a couple of shacks tucked in alongside the roadway.

As you approached the intersection of the Old Jay Hill Road, Sanborn's turkey farm sat on the left. It was the one place everyone would go to at Thanksgiving time to purchase a fresh "Tom" for their holiday table. The fields were full of turkeys at this time of year. They scurried around for food, totally unaware of their upcoming fate that was just several months away. Dave slowed the truck down as Billy stuck his head out the window and made a loud gobbling sound. The turkeys all responded with the same loud sound of their own. "Sure are noisy," he said with a chuckle.

The truck turned right and headed towards town. There were a lot more houses along this stretch as they crossed the tracks and approached the four corners in the center of town. Once you cross through the four-way stop, the Grange store sat on the left. One lonely red gas pump sat by itself in the front of the store, the only place to fill up in town. The Grange was also the home for the local post office. The next building down from the Grange was the Town Hall, followed by the Methodist Church, and then the library. Just across from the church was the small schoolhouse that the boys attended. That was the extent of downtown. Once you passed the school and library, you were headed out of town. Dave pulled his truck up alongside the gas pump, shut off the engine, and stepped out. "You boys stay put. I'll be right back."

George Lane, owner of the Grange, was already out at the pump, nozzle in hand. "Fill her up?" He asked as Dave stepped out of the truck.

"Yup," Dave's replied. Dave walked back towards George, exchanged a couple of words, and then walked into the store. George finished pumping the gas and headed in.

About 10 minutes later, Dave came out carrying two small brown bags. He had been talking with George. He opened the door and stepped up into the truck. "Wow, look at that!" He exclaimed, pointing through the windshield.

Coming down the road, from the direction of the school, was a brand-new 1957 Chevy. It was red and white, with its snout nose shining from all the chrome. The fins on the back rose up off the car like the back of two sharks. It was a beauty! The driver turned in and pulled up on the other side of the gas pump. The three of them just sat there for a minute looking at the Chevy and talking about its style and design, pointing at the car as they spoke.

"Saw a picture of one in the Saturday Evening Post at home," Billy remarked. "First one I ever seen around here."

"Me too," Dave replied. "Oh, I almost forgot." He tossed one of the small brown bags into each of their laps. "Thought you might like a little treat."

The boys opened the bags as Dave started his truck and back out onto the road to head for home. He had purchased some penny candy for each of them while he was in the store. Inside the bags were squirrel nuts and Mary Jane's. Squirrel nuts were small rectangle pieces of chewy chocolate, with chopped nuts mixed throughout the piece of candy. The Mary Jane's were peanut butter flavored nougat, just a little bigger than the squirrel nuts, with real peanut butter inside. They were two of the most popular candies at the store and were the favorites of both Billy and Jake.

"Hey, thanks Uncle Dave," both boys echoed.

"One piece for now, save the rest for later," Dave said. "Don't need your mother mad at me for ruining your supper." They all laughed.

The rest of the day took a normal path right through bedtime. The boys were just getting ready to fall asleep when Billy whispered over to Jake, "We need to get the cigar box up to the treehouse."

"Okay," Jake responded with a mumble.

Billy quietly rolled out of bed, walked to the window and opened it about six inches. It was a warm night and any breeze would be welcomed through the bedroom window. "Nite, Jake," he said softly. There was no response from his brother. He climbed back to bed and slowly fell asleep to the sound of a whip-poor-will somewhere off in a distant tree.

During the night, Billy's mind took him into a dream about the bank robberies. Just as the shootout was taking place, there was a loud thunderous boom. He sat straight up in bed and yelled, "LOOK OUT!" He looked around and squinted toward the window. There were multiple flashes of lightning followed by more loud rolling thunder. A storm had snuck in during the night, not an uncommon event for a hot July evening.

As he started to get out of bed to close the window, he heard the bedroom door open. It was his mom. She switched on the light and whispered, "Eerything okay in here?"

"It's okay, mom," Billy said. "Thunder jumped me, that's all."

"I thought I heard someone yell."

"I guess it was me, Jake's still sleepin'."

"He's just like your father," she replied back." Sleep through anything. You and me, we hear it all."

Billy walked over and closed the window. The storm had passed quickly and he could see some stars peeking through the broken clouds. He turned, and jumped back to bed.

"Still got a few hours, get back to sleep," Sophie said as she flicked off the light.

"Nite, mom." She closed the bedroom door and he could hear her footsteps headed back down towards his parents' bedroom. "Funny how them dreams are," he muttered as he faded back to sleep.

Morning came quickly. The boys were already up finished with breakfast. They help their mother clear the table and headed outside. Billy was excited because today was the day they hoped to get the cigar box up to the treehouse. "We're going up to the treehouse, mom," Billy yelled to his mother.

"Okay," Sophie answered from the kitchen. "Just be careful and watch out for your brother." Jake had strapped on his holster and guns and was ready for some serious cowboys and Indians. As they entered the yard, Dave was working on the wood pile near the shed. The boys headed toward him.

"Hey, Billy!" Dave shouted. "Could you grab my work gloves from the truck. They're right on the floor in the middle."

"Sure," Billy said as he dashed over to the truck. He opened the door and leaned in along the seat. The gloves were right where Uncle Dave had indicated. As he started to reach for them, he noticed the ashtray sticking out from the dashboard. Inside were several half smoked cigarette butts. He hesitated for a moment, then picked one out from the back and cupped it in his hand. He reached down and grabbed the gloves, stepped back out of the truck and closed the door. He proceeded to take the gloves over to Dave.

"Thanks," Dave said as he pulled a small log from the pile. "Set them right there on the block."

Billy set the gloves down on the chopping block. "Gotta get some stuff for the treehouse out of the barn. Wait here, Jake. I'll be right back."

He ran into the barn and up into the loft to retrieve the cigar box. When he got to the wall, he un-cupped his hand and looked at cigarette butt he had taken from the truck. "I'm almost 14," he thought. Kids at school had already told him how they had tried it. "Nothin' to it," they had told him. He might try it, he might not. He stepped up onto a bale of hay, reached up and tucked the cigarette butt in the corner where one of the big beams met the wall. "No one will find it there," he thought. Reaching in behind the bales, he found the cigar box and pulled it out. As he exited the barn, he headed straight for the clothesline so that Dave could not see the box he was carrying. With the box tucked tightly under his arm, he yelled, "Let's go, Jake!"

Dave waved as Jake scampered towards Billy. "Have fun boys."

Jake waved back and Billy yelled, "See you later!" They walked into the field and headed up toward the treehouse. Dave watched them as they left the yard. He could see that Billy was carrying something under his arm, but he could not make out what it was.

As soon as they were on the platform Billy sat down cross legged and placed the cigar box in front of him. Jake was lying down facing out towards the pasture pretending to shoot Indians that were attacking his fort. Billy opened the box, took out the paper and spread it opened in his lap. He sat there studying it, his head moving side to side to give him different angles. It looked like an igloo with a squiggly bottom. At a different angle, it looked like a camels hump. What were these initials in the top corner? SM! Maybe it was the initials of the third man that Dave had talked about. He looked at all the little lines and the other writing that was on it. What was the "N" and arrow? What does 3TR mean? Nothing made sense.

He pulled himself to his knees and reached into his pocket. There was nothing there! It was gone! He checked his other pockets. There was just his knife and a piece of the candy that Dave had given them the day prior. The smaller first paper that Jake had discovered was nowhere to be found.

Jake let out a yell, "THEY GOT ME!" He rolled over and grabbed his shoulder as if the Indians had shot him. His feet swung around. kicked the side of the cigar box and it went flying off the platform and landed on the rocks below. When it hit, the box shattered into a dozen different pieces. Billy and Jake peered over the edge of the platform at the pieces below.

Billy had a disgusted look on his face. "Great!" He said, shaking his head.

"Just a dumb box," Jake replied.

"Yeah, yeah. Hey, you seen the other paper? Thought I had it but it ain't in my pockets."

"Nope, you said you were gonna to keep it." Jake went back pretending while Billy tried to think about the last time they looked at the first paper. He recalled checking it when they had found the markers on the stalls in the barn. That was a couple of weeks ago. He hadn't thought much about it since they discovered the cigar box. Maybe he dropped it in the barn. He would have to check for it later.

"Wanna play?" Jake asked as he ducked away from some imaginary arrows.

"In a minute," Billy replied. He wanted to look at the new paper one more time. He sat there and studied it again. Maybe it's a map. It could be anything. He looked up at Jake. "I think we should tell dad. What if it really is something? Maybe a grown-up could figure it out."

"He'll just be mad at us because we didn't tell him sooner," Jake commented "Hey, let's tell Uncle Dave! Maybe he can help us figure it out or tell dad that he found it, that way we won't get in trouble."

"That's not a bad idea," Billy responded. "I'll think about it." He stood up, folded the paper flat and slid it into his back pocket. It should be safe there. He'd be sure to keep a closer eye on this one.

Billy and Jake spent the rest of the morning playing at the treehouse before heading back to the house for lunch.

The Confession

Saturday came in no time at all. It was 5 am and Billy had already dressed, eaten breakfast and was standing impatiently by the front door. Sophie walked over and handed him a brown bag and thermos. "I packed you some lunch and lemonade," she said as she handed them to him.

He was waiting on Timmy Cutler and Timmy's dad. They were picking him up go fishing over at Wilson Lake in Wilton. Timmy's uncle had just gotten a brand-new motorboat and was meeting them at the lake. They would be spending the whole day drifting around on the lake trying to haul in some big ones. What more could a kid ask for than to spend the day out on a beautiful lake fishing with his best friend. Billy looked up as a black pickup pulled into the yard. There was a quick honk of the horn and Billy said, "They're here, mom. See ya."

"Have fun. Don't fall in," she said, jokingly.

He grabbed his gear next to the steps and tossed his stuff into the bed of the pickup. He climbed into the cab next to Timmy, said hello to Mr. Cutler and started telling Timmy about the fifty-seven Chevy that he had seen down at the Grange store.

"Mornin' Sophie," Mr. Cutler yelled as she stood in the doorway. "How's Josh doin'?"

"Mornin', Ralph," she replied. "He's doin' just fine, I'll tell him you was askin'."

They exchanged waves as he backed out of the drive and headed for Wilton.

Dave was awake, heard the horn beep, rolled out of bed, dressed and came downstairs. Sophie was still standing in the doorway. She turned to walk back into the house. "David!" She said, in a startled voice.

"Didn't mean to sneak up on you," he said smiling.

"You're up a bit early this mornin'. Want some breakfast?" She asked.

"I'm just gonna' have some cereal. I'll fix it." He walked over to the cupboard, grabbed a bowl and the box of cereal. On the way by, he pulled the pitcher of milk out of the refrigerator and proceeded on to the table. As he sat down at the table, he looked over at Sophie. "Hey, Soph, do you think the boys have been acting a little strange lately?"

"Can't say I noticed anything. Why?"

"Oh, it's just a feeling I got. Like they had something cooking, but didn't want anyone to know."

"Just boys being boys," she responded. "Probably ain't no big deal."

"Yeah, I guess you're right," Dave said. He decided to change the subject so he and Sophie finished breakfast talking about the upcoming Farmington Fair. Dave knew that Billy was gone for the day so he would try to pick a good time to see if he could get any information out of Jake. Maybe it really wasn't anything at all. He had seen some puppies in Wilton, and had thought about getting one for the boys. Maybe he could use that to get some conversation going with Jake.

The opportunity came in early afternoon. Jake had been chasing the cats around in the barn. Dave was chopping wood when Jake came out of the barn and headed for the house. "Hey, Jake, got a minute?" Dave said, motioning him over.

"Sure, what's up?" Jake asked.

"I'm gonna' tell you a secret, but you have to promise not to say a word to anyone."

"Okay!" Jake said. "I promise." He put his finger up to his chest and made the X sign. "Cross my heart."

"Okay. Well, I think I'm gonna' get you guys a dog. Your mother told me that you lost your last one a year ago when he got hit by a car."

"Wow, really? We asked dad a while back about gettin' one. He said he'd see about it. You know what kind it would be?"

Dave smiled, "Yup, it's a beagle. They got some puppies over in Wilton. Just about ready to leave their mother. But you can't say anything. I gotta talk to your dad first to make sure it's okay."

"I won't tell, I promise," Jake stated.

"So," Dave said quickly. "You got any secrets you want tell me?"

Jake was silent for a few seconds. "Nope," he mumbled, looking at the ground.

"Aw, come on," Dave prodded as he put his hand on Jake's shoulder. "You don't have any secrets at all?"

Jake looked up the Dave. "Yeah, I got one, just can't tell ya, that's all."

"Well, I trusted you with my secret. And I promise I won't tell a soul." Dave made the cross my heart sign on his chest.

"If Billy finds out he's gonna' kill me!" Jake blurted out.

"I promise I won't tell him."

"Okay," Jake said hesitantly. "This all started a while back." Jake began explaining to Dave about finding the jar with the paper in it. He described how the paper had letters and numbers all over it. Some of the letters match the bank robber's names, but he couldn't remember the other stuff on it. He told Dave, how they had found the markers on the stalls and then found the cigar box in the stall. There wasn't a lot of detail to his story, so Dave was trying to piece things together as Jake rambled on. Could it just be a tall tale that they made up together while playing cops and robbers? Dave was absolutely clueless at this point.

"Wow!" Dave said, when Jake was finished. "That's quite a secret. So, where are the papers now? Did you guys hide them again?"

"No," Jake replied. "I think Billy lost the first one, but he still got the one from the cigar box. No telling, right? You promised."

"Right, you too," Dave answered as he patted Jake on the shoulder.

"Right," Jake agreed.

"Want to help me lug some wood into the shed?"

"Okay." Jake helped Dave for the next hour or so before heading back into the house.

Dave couldn't stop thinking about everything that Jake had told him. What if they really had found something important? What if it was some kind of clue to where those fellas put the stolen money? Now, he'd have to get Billy to tell him about it without squealing on Jake. He laughed to himself, knowing that he would think of something.

Mr. Cutler and Timmy dropped Billy at home around eight thirty that evening. He waved goodbye as they headed back down the hill. He took a minute to put his fishing gear in the shed. He walked into the house, carrying a big stringer of lake trout held high over his head. Everyone had already eaten and was sitting in the living room, engaged in conversation, as he walked in. Josh looked over from his chair as Jake ran towards Billy to get a better look at the fish. "Um, um," Josh said. "That's a mighty fine lookin' string ya gut there!" Dave was nodding in agreement.

"Thanks," Billy said, grinning.

"Get them to the sink so they don't drip everywhere!" Sophie yipped. "Are you hungry? We already had supper."

"Yeah, a bit," Billy replied.

"There's a pot of goulash on the stove. You can grab some when you're done cleaning them fish. I'll fix you up some bread and butter to go with it."

Dave got up from the couch and headed into the kitchen. "I'll clean them up for you. Go ahead and eat."

"Thanks, Uncle Dave," Billy responded. He laid them on some newspaper next to the sink as Dave came into the kitchen. After washing his hands, he grabbed a plate out of the cupboard and ladled out a big helping of mom's famous goulash from the pot.

Just as Billy sat down to eat his supper, Josh bellowed out from the living room, "Tha fair starts this comin' Thursday! Been a slight change in plans. Everett wants ta take ova five or six a them milkers this year, plus all tha equipment. I'm gonna' need some help gettin' ready fa tha next few days. Billy en Jake, I'm gonna' need ya ta help me. That okay?"

Jake was in the kitchen watching Dave clean the fish. He couldn't believe his ears. He swung around towards his dad with his mouth hanging almost the floor. "ME TOO, DAD?" He shouted.

"Yup, you too," came the reply.

Jake started dancing around the kitchen making a high-pitched, woo hoo, woo hoo sound while throwing his hands up in the air. Finally, he was being asked to help. His delight was obvious. "Calm down, son!" Josh yelled. "Ya gonna' break a leg, then ya won't be no help at all."

"Jake, calm down," Sophie said in a laughing whisper as he tried to grab him around the shoulders.

"I ain't finished yet!" Josh yelled again. "Since we're gonna' have so many cows at tha fair, I told Mr. Robinson I was gonna' need help tendin' to em. He said you two boys would do just fine. So, you're gonna' be ova there with me all four days. That's OKAY, right?" He was grinning ear to ear.

Billy was nodding, still chewing on his supper. Jake was still trying to dance as Sophie held on.

Josh still wasn't finished. "Oh yeah, one more thing. Mr. Robinson said since you'll be doin' all tha work, he's gonna' pay for all them carnival rides en games for ya."

Jake stops short in his tracks and Billy stopped chewing and stared at his dad. They couldn't believe what they had just heard. Jake was thrilled about finally getting to work with his dad and now this too. It was a dream come true. Billy thought differently about it. It would be the first time he would be getting paid to work or at least to him it was like pay. He was becoming the second man of the house.

"Hey, Dave, I'd be happy ta have ya come ova en help to, if ya like."

"Thanks, Josh," Dave replied. "Think I might. I'd like that."

There wasn't a happier house on the 'Hill' that night as they all prepared to go to bed. There'll be a lot to do between now and Thursday.

Sunday was the only day of the week that Josh didn't stay all day at the dairy. He would go in for the morning and evening milking, but the rest of the day was his. Services were always at ten o'clock sharp at the Beans Corner Baptist Church followed by Sunday school. Once they finished up, it was back home by noon for their Sunday lunch.

Jake had headed up to his room after lunch was over. Everyone was in the living room talking about the fair. Dave had come up with a plan on how to talk with Billy about the papers that the boys had found. Earlier that day, Sophie had asked Dave if he could check the rope swing in the barn to make sure it was safe for the boys to swing on.

He tapped Billy on the shoulder. "Hey, Billy, your mom wants me to check out that rope swing you boys have in the barn. Think you could help me with that?"

"Yeah, sure. I'll race ya," Billy replied.

"Okay, will be back in a bit," Dave said as he turned and looked at Sophie. He and Billy darted out through the sheds and into the barn. Dave followed Billy up into the loft. He walked over and sat down on a bale of hay, breathing a little heavier than normal. "Must be getting old," he muttered to himself.

"That's the rope right up there," Billy said as he pointed to the high beam in the top of the loft.

"I know," said Dave. "Before we look at it, I need to talk to you."

Billy turned towards him with a curious look. "About what?"

"Well, I figured you might have something you wanted to tell me."

Billy stood silent for several moments, his mind racing. How did he know? How did he find out? Billy's thoughts were everywhere. He could feel the panic building up inside. His lip was quivering as he started to speak. "I........, I'm sorry Uncle Dave," he blurted out, his voice stammering a bit. "I know I shouldn't of took it. I just saw them in the ashtray when I went to get your gloves, so I took one. I didn't smoke it, honest. It's hid right there." He pointed back towards the wall as he rushed past Dave. He jumped up on the bale of hay and retrieved the cigarette butt.

Dave was a little stunned, but didn't say a thing. He watched Billy and thought to himself, "Well I'll be. This boy is confessing something that nobody even knows about." Dave was chuckling inside. He wasn't quite sure how to handle the situation. Billy returned, his hand shaking as he held out the cigarette butt. Dave could see that he was scared.

"Please don't tell dad. He'll kill me!" Billy pleaded.

"That's fine, just calm down. Sit down here," Dave said pointing to the bale of hay next to him. As Billy sat down, Dave put his arm around his shoulder. "Now, why did you go do something like that?"

"Cause, the kids in schools said they all done it already. I thought I would try it, but I didn't," Billy responded with still a little fear in his voice.

"Well, I'm not gonna' tell your folks, okay? Only because you didn't do anything with it. Just don't do something stupid like that again. Besides, they're not good for you."

"Then how come you smoke them?"

"Guess I'm stupid, too," Dave answered with a little laugh. Now he had Billy a little relaxed and smiling. He knew that he could get all the information he wanted now that he knew about the cigarette incident. He thought for a second about what would be the best way to start talking about the papers. "You know," he said looking at Billy. "I've noticed you and your brother acting a little strange over the past few weeks. Then I saw you carrying that little box up to the treehouse. I figured there was something up, I just couldn't figure out what it was."

Billy remained silent, still looking at Dave.

"So," Dave continued, "I tricked your brother into telling me about the papers you found. His story wasn't very clear, so I thought you could fill me in on exactly what was going on."

"What a blabbermouth!" Billy said.

Dave's voice became serious. "Now listen up. You can't let your brother know that I talked to you about it. I promised him I wouldn't tell anyone. You can tell him you told me, that way he won't know that I asked you about it. I don't tell your folks about the cigarette, you don't tell your brother about this. AGREED?" He stuck his hand out to Billy.

Billy slowly moved his hand over and shook Dave's hand. "Okay," Billy said. "But he's still a blabbermouth." After a slight hesitation, Billy asked, "did you know I took that cigarette butt?"

Dave smiled. "Nope, not till you told me." He chuckled as Billy sat there shaking his head, his bottom lip curled down. "Anyway, why don't you tell me all about the papers you found."

Billy proceeded to tell Dave about the same events that Jake had described to him except Billy had much more detail to the story. You could see as Billy went on that Dave was becoming more and more interested in what they had found. When Billy described the initials that were on the first paper, Dave interrupted. "You sure the initials on the paper matched up Sam Green and Frank Walker?"

"Yeah, I'm sure," Billy answered. "It was SG and FW, and there was another one. I think it started with a T, just can't remember. I know that on the bottom was ST-2 Left Side." He went on to explain to Dave about finding the horse stall markers and finding the cigar box on the left side of the stall number two, hidden up on the beam. He finished up his tale by telling Dave about how they took the cigar box to the treehouse to study the new paper. He also explained how Jake had kicked the cigar box off the platform and it had smashed to pieces on the rocks. "Since then we ain't had much time to look at the paper," he concluded.

"Where are the papers now?" Dave asked.

"Don't know what happened to the first one. I lost it. Been looking everywhere but can't find it. I got the big one right here." Billy stood up, reached into his back pocket slid out the folded paper.

Dave had a surprised look on his face. He didn't think he would be getting to see it quite this quickly. "Let's take a look," he said in a hurried voice.

Billy sat down and unfolded the paper, holding it over towards Dave. "We can't make no sense of it," Billy said. "What do you think?"

Dave looked it over for a minute or two. It was just as Billy had described. The initials SM were on the top, the letter

N with an arrow pointing up next to it, and TR3 on the right with the words 100 feet written under it. The semi-circle, with a squiggly dotted line along the bottom filled the rest of the paper. "Looks like a mushroom head with a jagged bottom," Dave commented. "And what the heck could this be?" He pointed to the small square near the top left of the semicircle. It had several little lines above it. "Boy, it sure doesn't make much sense," Dave said as he continued to study the paper. "Do any of these letters or numbers match up with the first paper?"

"Nope," Billy said, emphatically. "Everything on this one is different than the small paper."

"Well, I guess it could be a map or something like it."

Just then Jake's voice sounded from the bottom of the loft ladder. "Billy, Uncle Dave, you up there?"

"Yeah Jake, come on up," Billy answered.

As he climbed onto the loft, Jake saw the paper opened on Dave's lap. He quickly looked at Dave and then over to Billy. "What are you guys doing?" He asked.

Billy hesitated for a moment as he looked at Dave. "I told Uncle Dave about what we found. Remember we talked about tellin' him the other day?

"Oh, okay," Jake said quietly. "Guess it's okay then. You guys figure it out yet.?"

"Nope, not yet." He looked over at Billy. "Is it okay if I keep it for a few days so I can study it more?"

"Sure," Billy replied. "You're gonna' give it back, right?"

"Sure thing," Dave answered.

"You ain't gonna' tell dad are you?" Billy asked, quickly.

"No, not yet. But we might have to if it turns out to be anything important. We'll just wait and see. Okay? Come on, let's get that rope checked out."

Billy and Jake nodded in agreement.

Farmington Fair

Josh and the boys had spent the last three days at the dairy, getting everything prepared. How could it have come so quickly? It was Thursday, August 1, the first day of the fair. The equipment was polished and shiny. "Like tha sun at high noon in July." The tractors, mowers, rakes, and all the milking equipment were ready for the fair. They also spent a lot of time grooming the cows that had been selected to go.

Mr. Robinson brought in two large trucks, the day prior, and everything was hauled over to the fairgrounds. They had followed the trucks in Josh's Pontiac, got everything in place, put the cows in the barn at the fairgrounds, and gave the chosen six an early milking. Fred and Skip would be staying at the dairy to tend the rest of the cows while Josh was away.

They returned home by early evening to get a good night's sleep. They would need it for the long four days ahead.

It was 3:30 am when the alarm clock broke the stillness of the night with its loud ring. Billy rolled out of bed, walked to the dresser and pushed in the small pin on the back of the clock. There was total silence. He walked over, turned on the light and approached Jake's bed. He placed both hands on the lump under the bedspread and rocked it back and forth. "Jake, wake up. We gotta get going. Dad will be mad if you don't get up."

Jake's head appeared from under the bedspread. He rolled over and opened his eyes. "Okay, okay, cut it out!" he said pushing Billy's hands away. "I'm up." He swung around and sat up on the edge of his bed.

Billy could hear his mom and dad in the hallway. Their door popped open and Sophie stuck her head in. "You boys up and ready?"

"Almost mom," Billy answered. "We'll be right down."

"Okay, let's skedaddle. Breakfast in five minutes. Don't keep your father waitin."

The boys finished dressing and headed downstairs. French toast and scrambled eggs was the morning menu, topped off with a cold glass of orange juice. As they hurried through breakfast, Josh spoke to the boys. "First thing we gotta do is feed em, then milk em down when we git there. Then you two just gotta keep an eye on em and keep em clean."

"No problem," Jake answered quickly

Billy just smiled and shook his head. He knew that they would be hand milking the cows this morning and Jake wouldn't have a clue as to what to do. There were several cows at the dairy that would not let you put the milking machines on them. One in particular was Rosie. She had a crippled leg and would kick up a storm when you tried to get near her with the milking machine. She had no complaints, however, about being milked by hand. Josh had taught Billy the proper way of hand milking and he had become quite good at it.

Sophie had packed their lunches the night before so everything was ready to go. She didn't plan to go over to the fair until Saturday. She followed them to the door where Josh turned and gave her a quick kiss goodbye. "See ya tanight," he said.

"Okay, Josh. Have fun boys," she yelled as they headed for the car. Jake hopped into the back seat, as Billy climbed into the front seat with his dad.

"You boys ready?" Josh shouted out.

"We're ready!" They yelled back in one voice.

"Here we go!" Josh bellowed as he pulled out of the drive and headed for Farmington.

The fairgrounds set on the outskirts of Farmington. There was a tall solid green wooden fence that surrounded the entire grounds. Behind these walls was the home of one of the largest agricultural fairs in the state of Maine. There were acres of parking area and row upon row of the barns that housed all the animals during the fair. The grounds also held a full-size horse racing track with grandstands. It was one of the fairs main attractions. It would be packed to capacity this weekend when the trotters were racing. There were also hundreds of areas for setting up equipment displays and the food vendors. The large carnival was set up on the right end of the grounds with its Ferris wheel, rising high above the fence. This gave everyone on board a full look over the entire area. The games, carnival shows, and the other rides were spread out around the Ferris wheel.

The competitions and judging would start today and continue right through Sunday. They would be sheep shearing, horse jumping, horse pulling, oxen pulling, and more. They would all be competing for the best of the best. First Place! The animal barns housed just about every variety of farm animal found in the state. Everywhere you looked there was something different.

It was still dark as Josh and the boys approached the fairgrounds. The boys could see the outline of the large Ferris wheel as it shot up from behind the big green fence. "Looks even bigger than last year," Jake said as he peered out through the back window.

"It's the same one," Billy answered.

Josh drove by the main gate, and headed around to the left side of the grounds. He would use the smaller entrance over there because it would keep them closer to the barns that housed the six cows from the dairy. As he pulled up to the entrance, there were two teenage boys tending the gate. Once inside, the second boy pointed to the area where he could park over near the barns. Josh found the closest open spot, pulled the Pontiac in, and shut it off. They exited the car and headed for the barns.

When they entered the barn, the cows were already standing up in anticipation of their morning feeding and milking ritual. This particular barn also held cattle from five other farms. There was a bustling of activity going on up and down the barn. The barns were all double sided with an extra wide walkway right down the middle. This was to allow the fair patrons the opportunity to walk through the barns and observe the animals in their respective areas.

"Let's feed em up," Josh said as he pointed to the hay and grain located at the back of the area. There were several holding tanks for milk between each cattle barn. The milking buckets were kept in a covered box in the corner. "I'm gonna' clean em and start milkin," he said to the boys. He went down the line wiping the milk sacks and udders to remove any foreign materials that could fall into the buckets as they were milking them. Billy and Jake started distributing the hay and grain as Josh retrieved a bucket and a small three-legged stool.

"When ya done, start on tha otha end!" Josh yelled. "Jake, you can help me down hea."

"Okay!" Billy yelled back.

Once they finished the feeding, Billy grabbed a bucket and stool and headed down to the last cow on the other end. Jake walked down to join up with his dad. Billy could hear Josh explaining and showing Jake how to do the hand milking. "Dad is such a great teacher and so patient," Billy thought as he remembered his first time.

Jake was excited and anxious to learn everything he could. After a few unsuccessful tries, he finally had some milk coming out into the bucket. As soon as Josh saw that Jake was comfortable at doing it, he said, "Okay, I'm gonna' set ya up on tha next one. Go git yaself a bucket en stool."

Jake was back in a flash and set the stool down near the next cow in the line. "Just do what I showed ya," Josh said. "You'll be just fine. It's easier than it looks."

As they finished each cow, the buckets were carried out and emptied into a holding tank. It would be picked up shortly and taken down to the breakfast shack for the fair workers. There's nothing better than fresh milk in the morning. Jake was just finishing up his first cow by the time that Josh and Billy had finished the rest. "How ya doin'?" Josh asked as he approached Jake.

"Okay, I guess," Jake said, sounding a little disappointed. "Just a little slow."

Josh placed his hand on Jake's shoulder. "It don't matter. It's ya first one. Probly twice as fast as my first one. Ya did a great job, son. Okay, now git that bucket empty. Then you en Billy take them buckets ova ta tha washroom en wash em good. I gotta git ova ta tha equipment display. I'll be back lata. If there's any problems come en git me."

After returning from the washhouse, Billy and Jake spent some time grooming and cleaning up after the cows. The boys then took turns walking up and down the barn introducing themselves to the farmers they didn't know.

Dave had promised Sophie he would take her grocery shopping over to the Red and White store in Wilton. He had told Josh that he would be over to the fairgrounds later in the day. He and Sophie had returned from the store just before noon and Dave carried all the bags into the kitchen. Sophie stood with her hands on her hips, staring at all the bags. "Thanks, Dave. Lord, I think I was out of everything."

"Okay, Soph. I'm gonna' head for the fair. I'll see you later."

"Byeee," Sophie chirped. "Tell them men of mine that I miss them."

"Will do." Dave returned to his truck and headed out of the drive and down the hill. He was going to the fair but first there was another stop he wanted to make. He drove into town and pulled up in front of the town hall. In a passing conversation, Josh had told him about Laura Jenkins. She was the lady who took care of all the business at the town hall and had the reputation of being the town gossip. "She knows more bout everyone round hea then they know bout themselves,"

Josh had told him. "Don't tell her nothin' ya don't want tha whole world ta know."

Dave walked in and approached the counter. Laura was seated at a desk in the back. She turned and looked at Dave as he came in. "Howdy, can I help you?" She pushed herself up from the chair. She was short, plump, and getting on in years. Her whole body swayed side to side as she walked towards the counter.

"Hi, I'm David Clough." That was as far as he got. Laura was off on a rant.

"Oh yes, heard all about you. Tough thing, divorce. At least there ain't no kids. Just makes it worse. Heard that Dustin boy is getting divorced too. Such a shame. Seems like more and more of them happening every day. How's your sister? Ain't seen her in a while."

"Wow," Dave thought to himself. Josh was right. She's a walking encyclopedia on everyone's business. He chuckled to himself.

"Sophie's doing great," he interjected quickly. "I'll tell her you were asking. I was wondering if you have any listings for people who lived around here back in forty-six?"

"Sure, we got them, but they ain't here," she replied. "Gotta go two doors up to the library. They keep them over there. God knows how far back they go. Just go in and ask for Anne. She'll show you right to them."

"Okay, thanks," Dave said as he turned quickly and hurried out the door. He didn't want to give her a chance to get going again. Once outside, he jumped into his truck and drove past the church and into the library parking lot. As he entered the library, he caught sight of a young woman with long, flowing auburn hair. She was kneeling down, putting books away on one of the shelves. She heard the door open, stood up, and watched him approach.

"Good afternoon," she said, politely. "May I help you with something?"

"Good afternoon to you, ma'am, you must be Anne," Dave replied. "I'm David Clough. I'm looking for the town registers for nineteen forty six."

"Those would be in our reference room, right over here," she responded very softly, as she started walking towards a small room on the other side of the library. "You must be new in the area. I've never seen you in here before."

"Yes Ma'am. I'm staying with my sister and her family up on Macomber Hill."

"Guess you haven't talked to Laura yet," Dave mumbled under his breath.

"What was that?" She asked.

"Oh, I was sayin' that Laura, at the Town Hall, sent me over. She said you kept all the records here."

"Yes, they're right here." She pointed to a shelf in the small room. "Just let me know if you need any help." She turned and walked out of the room.

"Hmmm. Blue eyes, auburn hair, and quite a looker," he said to himself.

He turned and searched the shelf for the 1946 town register. Once he located it, he slid it out from the shelf and took it over to a small table. Reaching into his back pocket, he took out the paper that he had gotten from the boys and sat down. He started going through the register and found a listing for Sam Green. Sam was born in 1912, which would have made him thirty-four years old at the time of the robberies. Sam's listed address was RFD 1, Macomber Hill Road.

"Well I'll be," Dave mumbled. "He lived right there on the 'Hill'."

Dave thumbed through to the W's where he found the name of Frank Wheeler. Frank was born in 1913 and lived on Perkins Road. He looked over at the SM printed in the top right corner of the paper and immediately flipped to the M section of the register. Only four last names beginning with M were listed: Theodore Munson, Joseph Metcalf, Harold Madison, and Eleanor Madison, Harold's wife. There was no one listed with the initials of SM. "If there was another person, they could have been from another area," Dave mumbled to himself. "I wish I had seen that first paper. I might have gotten something from it."

He closed the book, returned it to the shelf, and walked back to the table. He picked up the paper, folded it, and slid it into his back pocket. As he headed back out past the librarians desk, he said, "Thanks Anne," in a quiet whisper.

She looked up at him and smiled. She whispered back, "You don't have to whisper. You can talk normal." Then in her normal voice she said, "Besides, we're the only ones here." Dave stops short and started to laugh. She laughed along with him.

"Did you find what you were looking for?" she asked.

"No, but I wasn't sure what it was I was looking for to begin with. Might have to stop by again."

"That would be fine. I'll see you next time."

"You have a nice day Anne," Dave replied.

"You also, Mr. Clough."

"You can call me Dave. Mr. Clough is my father," he said with a chuckle. He reached out to shake her hand.

She responded and said, "Okay, bye Dave."

He left the library still smiling as he headed toward his truck. He threw his keys up and flicked them out of the air with his hand. "Cute as a button," he said out loud. "Guess I just might have to come back." Dave stepped into his truck and backed out of the parking lot. The next stop would be the Farmington fairgrounds.

The main gate of the fairgrounds opened at 10 am and people started flooding in. The larger crowds would start arriving around 6 pm. There was always something enchanting about being at the fair after darkness had set in. The noise of the carnival, the lights and music, cotton candy, french-fries and caramel apples would all fill the night air with intoxicating sounds and smells.

The boys knew that their father would be spending most of his days showing of the equipment they had brought from the dairy. His display was a good distance from their barn, in the direction of the carnival. Their responsibility was pretty cut and dry. Tend to the animals, be polite to everyone coming through the barn, and answer any questions they could. "Don't fagit ya Sirs en Ma'am's," Josh had told them. If any serious problems should occur, they were to fetch their father as fast as they could. Josh had written down some facts and figures to help the boys answer certain questions about the cows and the dairy farm, should they be asked. They had both been studying the list throughout the morning. The boys were a little nervous as the crowd started coming through. Most of the questions were pretty easy to answer and the boys became more and more relaxed as the day went on.

"What type of cows are they?"

"How much milk do they make?"

"How much do they eat?"

"How many cows are at the dairy?"

At times, it was just one or two people stopping to look. As it got busier, there would be a dozen or more looking and asking questions. It was early afternoon and there were about ten people standing in front of their area. A young woman with two small girls stepped up to the front of the group.

"My daughter would like to know how much milk your cows make," she said politely.

"Yes ma'am," Billy replied. "These cows give about six gallons of milk a day. If you add that all up with the number of cows we have at the dairy, they make about three hundred and forty thousand gallons of milk a year."

You could hear a couple of "WOWS" from the onlookers.

The cow at the far end let out a long "Mooooooooo."

One of the little girls looked up at Billy and asked, "How come cows moo?" He didn't even hesitate with the answer. "It's because their horns don't work." Everyone started laughing. He had gotten that one straight from his dad. As the crowd started to move on, they waved and said thank you, still chuckling as they left.

"Thanks for stoppin'!" Billy yelled, as he and Jake waved back.

Dave arrived at the fair around 2 pm. Josh had gotten him a pass for his truck and he entered through the side gate. After a little searching, he found the boys at the barn. They were feeding and watering the cows as he came in. "Hey boys," Dave said as he approached the area.

"Uncle Dave, you made it," Billy replied.

"Hi," Jake said giving a quick wave.

"Where's your dad?" Dave asked.

"He's over showin' the equipment," Billy said, pointing out through the end of the barn. "It is quite a ways down headed towards the carnival."

Dave motioned for the boys to come over to him. "I did some checking on those initials on the paper," he told them in a subdued voice. "I went to the library to look them up. Didn't come up with anything. I'm gonna' keep checking, okay?"

"Okay," the boys both nodded.

"I'm gonna' go give your dad a break, then I'll get back here." Dave headed out of the barn in search of Josh and the equipment display. Josh returned to the barn about fifteen minutes later to have lunch with the boys before returning to the equipment area. Dave spent the afternoon helping out between both areas and filling and in when someone needed a break.

The second milking of the day took place around 5:30 pm with a good size crowd watching them. Their day at the fair ended around 10 pm and they headed home. Jake and Billy both dozed off on the way home. They would be back at the fair before 5 am the next morning.

Friday was pretty much a replay of Thursday, except Dave followed them over in the morning and spent the whole day with them.

Carnival Time

The boys had been looking forward for Saturday to arrive. Come early evening, they would be headed to the carnival with their mother to enjoy the rides and games. Dave would be bringing Sophie over in the afternoon and she would stay for the rest of the day. She always looks forward to it every year. Her quilt would be sold at the auction tonight, but her biggest thrill was the Ferris wheel. She had loved the ride ever since she was a kid. It was the only ride she would go on and it had become a tradition for her, Jake, and Billy to go on the ride together. Dave had already told the boys that he would tend to the animals so they could have time to enjoy the carnival.

Josh walked down alongside the barns toward the equipment area. He had just had lunch with the boys back at the barn. Dave was watching the display. He would be headed back to the 'Hill' to pick up Sophie as soon as Josh returned. Josh could hear the shouting from the grandstands as he passed the racetrack. "The trotters must be runnin'," he thought to himself. It was a beautiful day and the fairground was becoming crowded with people. Danny Fuller was just getting his team ready for pulling as Josh came up on the horse pulling area. He stopped to watch for a minute. There were so many people lined up along the fence that he really couldn't get a good look at Danny and his team. He heard Danny yell "Har" and could hear the snort of the horses as they lurched forward. The heavy chains, attached to a large sled loaded with granite slabs, made a snapping noise as they tightened from the pull of the horses. You could hear the sled dragging its metal plated runners along the ground. "Go git em," Josh muttered as he turned and continued on towards the equipment display.

"I'm all set," Josh said as he walked up to Dave.

"Okay Josh. I'm headed out to get Soph. Be back in a bit." Dave walked off towards the parking area to find his truck.

The boys started cleaning and grooming the cow's right after Josh left them. The judges would be coming through shortly and everything had to be in tip top condition. Mr. Robinson came into the barn just as the boys were cleaning up.

"Hey Billy," he spouted. "Where's ya pa?"

"Hi, Mr. Robinson," Billy answered. "He's down with the equipment. It's on the other side of the fair headed towards the carnival."

"Heard rumors you boys were doin' a heck of a job around here!" He gazed up and down the row of cows. "The girls are lookin' mighty fine today, mighty fine!"

"Thanks, we're all set for the judging. They should be by here any time now," Billy responded.

"I'm goin' over ta see your dad," Mr. Robinson said as he turned to head back out of the barn. He stopped and turned back towards the boys. "Oops, almost forgot," he said as he reached into his pocket and pulled out some crumpled dollar bills. He motioned him over and handed them two dollars each. "Mighty fine," he repeated again. "Your folks should be real proud. You boys have fun at the carnival."

"Wow, thanks Mr. Robinson, we sure will!" Billy said with excitement in his voice.

"Yeah, thanks," Jake echoed.

Mr. Robinson left to find Josh as Jake and Billy started dancing around in a circle, holding them money up in the air. "We can go on every ride and play every game out there!" Jake shouted to Billy.

"Excuse me," said a voice from the middle of the barn. "Is this the Robinson Dairy area?"

Billy turned to see three men standing in front of their area holding notepads and papers in their hands. It was the judges. "Yes sir," Billy said pointing to the Robinsons Dairy sign hanging from the front of the area.

"We're ready to look at your cows and inspect your area," one of the men said.

"Yes sir, we're ready too," Billy replied with a big smile.

The men proceeded to wander through, checking everything. They looked at the feeding area, milk buckets, bedding, and checked on the cleanliness of the area. Once they finished with that, the cows were next. They began to check each one. They look at the legs, tails, milk sacks, udders, eyes and teeth. They finally finished up and made a few last notes on their pads of paper. They thanked the boys for their time then went on to the next area. One of the men gave the boys a thumbs-up and a wink as he left the area.

"Did we win!" Jake asked Billy.

"Hope so. Won't know till tomorrow," Billy answered. "They gotta check all the other farms then they pick out the best."

Dave returned with Sophie around 3 pm. She delivered her quilt to the auction tent and went to spend some time with Josh. A little while later she joined Jake and Billy at the barn but they would not be going to the carnival until the evening milking was finished. Sophie stood towards the back of the area and watched her two young men greet the onlookers and answer questions. She thought again of how fast they had grown up and was impressed with how well they handled the questions being asked. She was so proud of them. After a while she called Billy over. "I'm goin' to see if I can find Mrs. Sheridan. Maybe she'd like to walk around the grounds for a bit."

"Okay mom, see ya later," Billy said as he walked back towards the front.

Dave spent most of his afternoon just wandering around the fairgrounds. He hadn't been to a fair in years so he was enjoying taking it all in. He would be relieving Josh around 6 pm. Josh had to go back to the barn to help the boys with the evening milking. Sophie finally met up with Mrs. Sheridan over near the auction tent. They strolled around the grounds, chatting and checking out all the activities that were going on.

At 6 pm, Dave arrived back at the equipment display. Sophie was already there with Josh. "Big crowd tanite," Josh said. "Ya gonna' be okay hea alone?"

"I'll be just fine," Dave answered.

"I'll be back in a while," Josh said as he and Sophie headed back to the barn to join the boys.

A lot of people stopped and watched as Josh and the boys went through the ritual of washing the cows down, grabbing their stools and milk buckets, and doing the hand milking. It was 7:30 pm by the time they had finished milking and cleaning. It would start getting dark within the hour and all the lights would be coming on throughout the fairgrounds.

"I betta git back ta Dave," Josh said. "You boys come git ya motha when Dave gits back hea."

Billy and Jake couldn't wait for Dave to return. The excitement of going to the carnival was building up inside them. As soon as Dave arrived at the barn, they headed straight out to meet up with their mother. They waved back at Dave as he yelled to them, "you boys have fun."

The carnival lights had just come on as Sophie and the boys walked towards them. There were hundreds of people, moving in every direction, enjoying the moment, young and old alike. The sounds and music were getting louder and louder as they got closer and closer. You could smell the aromas of the food stands and hear the yells of the carnival workers as they tempted people to try they ride or game. The first thing Jake did was to buy a caramel apple. He had waited all week for this special treat. Billy was trying his luck at knocking over some milk bottles with a baseball. They walked up and down between the rides and games, stopping along the way to try out different ones. Sophie would wait until they were through with each one. Then she would walk along with them until they decided to try another.

"Step right up! Ring the bell!" the carnival man was yelling. "Win a prize. How about you, son?" He was pointing at Billy.

"Sure, I'll give it a try," Billy answered. He handed the man a nickel and picked up the large rubber sledge hammer.

"Just hit right down on that platform and show us how strong you are!" the man yelled.

Billy held the hammer high over his head and brought it down as hard as he could. There was a large thump when it hit and a small metal ball shot up a tube towards the bell. It went about three quarters of the way up, stopped, and fell back to the bottom. Billy sat the hammer down and walked back towards his mother with a disgusted look on his face.

"Who's next, step right up! Ring the bell!" the man continued yelling.

"That was a great try," Sophie said, putting her arm around his shoulder. "What do you say we head for the Ferris wheel. I'm startin' to get excited about gettin' on there."

The line for the ride was fairly long, but it didn't matter. Sophie would have waited the rest of the night just to get on that ride. They kept inching closer and closer and finally they were next in line to be seated. The man moved a small chain that blocked the entryway to the ramp and they walked up to the loading platform. A second man held the bucket as they got in. Sophie sat in the middle as the boys pushed in beside her. The bucket was swaying back and forth as the man pulled the safety bar down in front of them to secure them into the seat. The bucket jerked ahead a little and then stopped to allow the next people in line to get aboard. Each time the wheel stop, the bucket would sway and they would be getting higher and higher off the ground.

Once all the buckets were full, the Ferris wheel went into full motion. It was a slow type motion and if you closed your eyes you would feel like you were floating. Round and round they went. From the top of the wheel you could see the entire fairgrounds, the lights of the city shining in the night, and scattered lights throughout the countryside. Sophie would point out different things each time they reached the top. She showed them the hospital where they were born, the lights from the church steeple, and the big bank building in the center of town.

Billy wondered if it was one of the banks involved in the robberies. "Got to get that paper back from Uncle Dave," he muttered to himself as a reminder. The wheel finally began to slow and then came to a complete stop. One by one, the buckets were emptied and refilled with new riders.

They hopped out onto the platform and walked back down the ramp. "OHHH, that was wonderful!" Sophie remarked. "I guess we better head back now. Hope you two had fun tonight."

Both boys had a little money left but they had seen and done just about everything they had hoped to do. "Yeah, I'm ready to go," Billy said.

"Me too," Jake said.

"Okay, we'll just stop and see your dad for a bit before we head back to the barn."

Josh was leaning up against one of the tractors looking a little tired. They could hear him singing Hank Williams, "Your Cheatin Heart", as they approached. The boys stopped and told him about everything they did and Sophie rambled on about the Ferris wheel ride. They finally made it back to the barn where Jake curled up on a bale of hay in the back and fell asleep.

Sunday was the breakdown day at the fair. There were still some final competitions going on and the carnival was in full swing until 5 pm. All of the animal showing and judging and been completed and it was time to get them loaded up and back to the dairy. Mr. Robinson came into the barn around 11:30 am.

"Them trucks should be here in half an hour," he said as he stood in front of the Robinson Dairy sign. "I sure like the looks of that," he said as he pointed at one blue and one red ribbon that were hanging from the bottom of the sign. A fair representative had come by earlier in the morning and put them there. They were for "Best Holstein Exhibit" (first place) and for "Best Jersey Exhibit," (second place). "We'll put them right up in the barn, right alongside the others," he boasted.

The big trucks were brought back in and by 12:30 the cows and equipment had been loaded and were on their way back to the dairy. "You boys make one last check. Make sure we don't forget nothin'," Josh told Billy and Jake. They scurried around, checking everywhere and everything. It was as clean as a whistle.

"All set dad," Billy said.

"Okay, let's git goin'," Josh announced.

They yelled their goodbyes to some of the others in the barn and after a few "See ya next years", headed for the car.

"Can't wait for next year!" Jake yelled as they pulled out of the fairgrounds. It had been four long days and they were all exhausted. It would be a great night for sleeping.

THE BUCKING BRONCO

What a week the last one had been! It was now Tuesday, August 6th. Dave and the boys had talked on Monday about making a trip to the mountain to go blueberry picking. They would probably make several trips over the next week or so to pick the berries before they dried up and were gone. Now was the best time to get them. Dave had mentioned to Sophie that he was going to go with the boys.

"Oh good," she said. "I was so worried about them goin' alone. I know they're growin' up, but I wish they'd slow down a bit."

Dave laughed. "They're both pretty responsible, Soph. Look what a good job they did at the fair."

"I know, I know," she said. "But I'm their mother, I'm supposed to worry."

Dave and the boys started out for the mountain about 10 am Tuesday morning. They were each carrying one of Sophie's big pots. "Don't you come back empty-handed," she joked as they started on their way.

They approached the brook about fifteen minutes later. Billy could hear the water, but it wasn't as loud as the last time he and Jake were there fishing. The weather had been hot and muggy over the past week or so and the water level had dropped. When they reached the bank, Billy looked upstream. "Good," he said to Dave. He pointed to the rocks that were now visible across the bed of the brook. "We can cross right there."

They formed a single file, work their way across the rocks, and stepped up onto the other side. Billy looked back and forth into the wooded area ahead. "There's a trail that goes up to the old loggin' road," he said as he headed towards an opening in the trees. "It's about half a mile or so to the field."

They followed the trail until they hit the logging road. From there, they proceeded on the road until they came to the base of the mountain. It was strange to see how all the trees became spruce trees, once you reach the mountain.

"Hey, Billy!" Jake yelled from up ahead. "Did you bring a bag?"

"Yeah, I grabbed one from the kitchen before we left," he answered pointing to his back pocket.

"Now what's that for?" Dave asked.

"Gotta get some spruce gum before we go back," Billy answered.

"Guess this is the place to get it," Dave said. "Haven't had any of that for years."

The gum that the boys were talking about was actually the sap that oozes out of the spruce trees. It would semi harden into small lumps on the bark of the trees. They would cut off the hardened pieces and take home a bagful. It had a slightly bitter taste and felt a little gritty when you first put it in your mouth. After a while, it would soften up and you could chew it, just like real gum!

"Which way now?" Dave asked.

Billy pointed. "Straight up. There's a small trail to follow. It'll take us right to the berries. You can take the trail right up to the top if you want. Dad took us up one time last year. Had to be real careful. It's pretty rocky up there."

It was a steep and steady incline as they trudged along through the trees. The spruce trees began to thin out as they moved further up the mountain. As they came out into the opening, Dave's eyes opened wide and he let out loud, "WOW!" Everywhere you looked were high-bush wild blueberry bushes, loaded with large ripe blueberries. Some of the blueberries were as big as his thumb. "This is amazing," he said in awe. "We'll take five minutes to rest a bit." They sat down near the edge of the field to relax. After a few minutes, Dave said, "okay boys, let's get picking! Shouldn't take long to fill these pots." He took a bag of sandwiches out of the pot he was carrying and set it next to a tree at the edge of the field.

While they were picking the berries, Billy asked Dave, "You gonna' give us back that paper we found?"

"I will," he assured him. "Just let me hold it for a bit longer. I want to check a few more things first. Okay?"

"Yeah sure," Billy agreed.

Dave stopped picking for a few minutes to look around the area. He gazed up toward the top of the mountain. Once you got to the top left side of the field, there was a small clump of trees. A small line of trees went across the top of the field and beyond that it started to get rocky. There was a mixture of small scrubby spruce trees and a rocky ledge that led all the way to the top. "Funny how nature builds things," he thought to himself.

They finished filling their pots in no time at all. Jake's mouth had turned blue from all the berries he had eaten while he was picking. They walked back to the edge of the field and set the pots down next to the tree where Dave had put the sandwiches. They sat on the ground and Dave distributed the sandwiches to Jake and Billy. After they finished eating, Billy and Jake took out their pocketknives and began searching out some of the trees that had good patches of spruce gum on them. Dave relaxed in the shade of the tree at the edge of the field. He leaned back against the tree with his hands behind his head and closed his eyes. It seems like an instant when he heard Billy say, "We're all set Uncle Dave. You ready to go?"

Dave opened his eyes and sat up. He had dozed off for a little bit and didn't even know it. "Yup," he responded. "Let's get these berries back to the house. Your mom's gonna' have her work cut out."

They gathered up the pots and headed for home. They were back at home in no time at all. They entered the house and took the berries into the kitchen. "I'll be right down!" Sophie yelled from upstairs.

The boys each grabbed a glass of lemonade and sat down at the table. Dave headed outside to have a smoke. Sophie came around the corner and into the kitchen. "How was the pickin'?" She asked.

Billy pointed to the counter. "Them bushes are packed with berries this year, mom. We were done in no time."

"Where's your uncle?" She said as she looked towards the living room.

"He went outside. Think he's havin' a smoke," Billy answered.

Sophie shook her head and curled up her lip. "Nasty habit," she muttered to herself as she walked over to the pots.

The rest of the day passed quickly. Supper was over and the boys had already gone to bed. Josh, Sophie, and Dave were sitting in the living room having a general conversation. "Either of you know anyone around here with the initials SM?" Dave asked.

Josh and Sophie looked at each other and thought for a moment. "Nope, can't say I do," Josh replied. Sophie was shaking her head side to side in agreement with him.

"How about a business or anything like that?

Sophie was still shaking her head and Josh replied, "Nope, not off hand. Whatcha looking for?"

"Oh it's nothing," Dave responded. He decided to change the subject before they started asking more questions. "I got another question," he said. "I know that the boys lost their dog last year. I want to get them another one, if that's okay with you."

"Oh, Josh, the boys would love that!" Sophie exclaimed.

"Well, they've been askin'. I just ain't had time ta look fa one." Josh replied.

"There's this beagle pup available over in Wilton. Believe it's a male. Pretty much house trained already. I could get it tomorrow," Dave stated.

"You go right ahead," Josh said. "That's mighty nice. The boys are gonna' be all excited when they find out." Josh continued talking. "We got us a wet spell comin' in. Three ta four days a rain. Nothin' heavy. Just a lotta wet. Hope it dries out by next week. We got tha second hayin' ta do.

"Well, I guess the boys won't be going berry picking for a few days," Dave said.

Sophie smiled. That was just fine with her. Dave stood up. "Past my bedtime," he chuckled.

"Mine too," Josh agreed. They all said their good nights and headed off to bed.

Dave lay in bed studying the paper. Maybe he was making too much out of this. He turned it over and over, then upside down. There was absolutely nothing on the paper that he could relate to the robberies. Why was he wasting his time at this? He laid paper on the table next to the bed. As he lay back to go to sleep he reminded himself not to forget to get the paper back to the boys.

The next morning, as Billy was feeding the cats in the shed, Dave walked up and handed him the paper. "I don't think it's much of anything. I'd hang onto it though, just in case something comes up".

"Okay," Billy answered.

Dave left the house to head for Wilton around 10 am just before the rain started to fall. It was just like Josh had said, "A nice slow and steady light rain". It was still enough to make it miserable outside. Josh had taken his lunch with him today, knowing that the rain was coming. The boys had been playing in and out between the house and the barn. Sophie was sitting on the couch listening to the big-band sounds on the radio and reading the Saturday Evening Post.

"Where is Uncle Dave gone?" Billy asked as he and Jake came running in from the shed.

She hesitated a bit before she answered. "Oh, I think he's gone lookin' for work again." She knew quite well where he was and what he was doing.

Dave had decided to stop by the library before heading over to Wilton. He was there for about an hour. He spent most of the time talking to Anne, although he had told her that he had stopped to look through the register books again. He suspected that she knew he had stopped by just to see her. They exchanged goodbyes and he headed for Wilton. When he finally arrived in Wilton, he went to the Red & White grocery and picked up a cardboard box and some dog food. When he returned to his truck, he took a small blanket that Sophie had given him, folded it, and placed it in the bottom of the box. Everything was ready and it was time to pick up the puppy at a home over near the Wilton Academy.

He arrives back home at 1:30 pm, pulled into the drive, and stepped out of his truck. The rain was still steady as he ran for the front door. He had left the box on the front seat of his truck. Sophie and the boys were in the living room when he entered. Sophie looked at him inquisitively, seeing he was empty handed. He nodded to her in a manner that told her his mission had been accomplished.

"Hey boys, pretty boring day, huh?" He said as he wiped his hands on his shirt.

"Yeah," they both responded.

"Well, you know what? Even the most boring days can turn out to be great days." Dave turned quickly and darted out the door. Both the boys had puzzled looks on their faces.

Billy looked at his mother and asked in a confused tone, "What's he doing?" Sophie shrugged her shoulders as if she was as confused as they were.

When Dave returned through the door, he was carrying the box under his arm. A small brown and white head, with its chin laid over the edge of the box, peered out into the room. The boys jumped up and rushed towards their uncle. The questions started flying.

"Is it ours?" "Can we keep it?" "Where did you get him?" "What kind is it?"

"Slow down, slow down!" Dave said as he sat the box down on the floor. "Let's see if I get all these right. It's a male Beagle. I got him over in Wilton. He's 10 weeks old and yes he's all yours. Your mom and dad said it was okay, so I pick him up today for you. He hasn't got a name yet. The two of you can pick one out."

Jake looked up at his uncle and smiled. Dave gave him a quick wink, knowing that Jake kept his promise and had never told his brother.

"Thanks, Uncle Dave!" Billy yelled as he picked the puppy out of the box. Sophie was patting his head as it squirmed, jumped, and wiggled in Billy's arms.

"He's so cute!" Sophie explained.

"He's like a little bucking bronco," Billy said as he tried to hold the pup still.

"Hey!" Jake yelled. "We can call him BUCKY!"

"That's a good one," said Sophie. Dave also agreed that it was a great name for the new pup.

"Okay, I like it too," Billy said nodding his head.

"Welcome to the family, Bucky," Sophie said as she shook his little paw and kissed him on the head.

"Let me hold him," Jake said to Billy.

Billy handed the pup to Jake. All the excitement and handling had taken its toll on Bucky. Jake felt something warm and wet on his arm. He held Bucky out away from him with both hands. "He's peein' on me!" Jake yelled.

They all started laughing. "He's just excited," Sophie remarked. "I'll get some towels then we can put him in the kitchen." She grabbed two towels from the kitchen, one for Jake and one for the floor. Once Jake was cleaned up, they took Bucky into the kitchen. He would be spending most of his time in here until he got used to his new home. Dave ran back to the truck and brought in the dog food.

It was a wet ending to the week. The rain lasted off and on through Friday night. The boys didn't seem to mind now that they had Bucky to preoccupy their time. They took him all through the house and the sheds and barn, letting him get acquainted with all the areas around his new home.

On Saturday, the boys headed out to the mountain to get more blueberries for their mother. This was the first time that they would be going alone. Sophie was a nervous wreck. She spent most of the time they were gone looking at the clock and talking to Bucky. "Oh, I hope they're okay," she would say looking at the pup. "What if something happens? I hope they don't get lost. You are not big enough to go find them. Where can they be? They should be back by now."

The boys returned by early afternoon when their pots full of berries. Sophie let out a big sigh of relief when she heard them coming in through the door. She didn't want them to know she had been worrying and watching the clock ever since they left. "Back already? She asked as they brought the berries into the kitchen. "I didn't even realize you'd been gone that long."

"It's a good thing Bucky can't talk," she chuckled to herself.

Like a Camels Hump!

The next week consisted of your typical summer days with nothing out of the ordinary happening. The sun had come out and dried the fields. They were mowed on Tuesday and raked and turned on Wednesday. Today, Friday, August 16th, the hay was being bailed and brought into the barns. A few loads will go up to the dairy to finish filling the lofts up there. The rest would be brought into the barn here at the house.

Dave had volunteered to drive one of the tractors that would be pulling the hay wagon. They brought the first load to the barn around 11 am. The right loft in the barn was empty, but there were still a few bales from last year on the left side. Before they could start unloading the new hay, the old bales were tossed down to the barn floor and stacked against the back wall. This would be used up first during the winter. Dave backed the hay wagon straight back into the barn. The bales were piled almost as high as the loft floor, so it was easy throwing them off onto the loft floor. Skip and Fred were there to help along with the boys. Dave and Skip started tossing the bales up onto the loft floor. They would fill the right side first. The boys were dragging the bales along the loft floor, helping Fred line them up against the back wall.

By 6:00 pm they had bailed, brought in and emptied their fifth and final load. The right loft was full and the left side was near capacity. The boys would be unable to use there Tarzan swing for a while. Dave pulled the empty hay wagon out of the barn. With Fred and Skip sitting on the back, he headed to the dairy to put the tractor and wagon back into the garage.

Billy and Jake pushed the sliding barn doors shut and walked out into the gravel driveway. "Want to go up to the fort?" Jake asked pointing up towards the treehouse.

"Maybe later," Billy replied. "I promised mom I'd checked the garden. She thinks some rabbits are diggin' under the fence and gettin' after everything. Wanna help?"

"Sure," Jake said. As they headed out past the barn Billy glanced up towards Spruce Mountain and thought about making another trip to get more berries for his mom.

"Go over the other side and check for holes under the fence," Billy said to Jake as he pointed across the garden. They both crawled along the garden fencing looking for any openings that would allow the rabbit's access to the garden. About halfway down, Billy leaned back on his heels and stared back at the mountain looming in the background.

Jake came around the corner and walked up next to Billy. "What are you doin'?" He asked.

"Just thinking about getting' more berries for mom," Billy replied.

Jake turned his head toward Spruce Mountain. "Don't it look like a big old camels hump?" he asked as he stared towards the top.

Billy's eyes opened wide as he stared harder at the mountain. "Jake!-----Jake! What did you just say?"

Jake started to repeat himself. "I said it looked...."

Billy jumped to his feet. "Yeah, I heard you, I heard you!" He reached into his back pocket, pulled out the paper and unfolded it. He looked back and forth from the paper to the mountain several times. "Jake, THAT'S IT!" Billy yelled.

"What's what?" Jake yelled back.

"It's the map.... I mean, it's the mountain. Looks like a camels hump. Just what I thought when we were up at the tree house. It's a map of the mountain. Look, look right here!" He held a map out towards Jake and traced the semicircle. "Look at them initials, SM. That must mean Spruce Mountain." He was getting excited as he pointed back towards the mountain. "See the area where the blueberry field is, while this is it!" He pointed down to the small square that was drawn on the map just below the semicircle.

Now they were both excited. "What do you think the dotted line is?" Jake questioned pointing to the bottom of the map.

"Well, if the square is the field, maybe it's the old loggin' road. What else we got down there?"

"That brook runs all the way along the bottom of the mountain!" Jake blurted out.

"You're right," Billy said. "I'll betcha it's the brook!"

Dave followed Fred and Skip into the barns from the garage. Josh had already started the evening milking and Fred and Skip would be helping him finish up. Dave was headed to the store for cigarettes and figured he'd asked Josh if he needed anything while he was there. Josh was just hooking up one of the cows to the milking machine as Dave approached him. "Hey Josh," Dave said. "All the hay is in and the tractor and wagon are back in the garage."

"Great," Josh replied. "Might git anotha small cut if tha weatha holds through Septemba."

"Let's hope it does. I'm headed to the store. Do you need anything?"

Josh glanced up at Dave wearing a big smile. "Guess ya must be, tha libraries closed this time a day." He winked at Dave. "Don't need nothin' at tha store."

Dave had a surprised look on his face. "Now how'd you know about that?"

"Oh, Sophie was talkin' ta Laura Jenkins tha otha day. Need I say more?" They were both laughing as Dave left the barn and headed for his truck.

Dave made a quick trip to the store and went straight back to the house. Both Billy and Jake looked back towards the barn as they heard Uncle Dave's truck pull into the gravel drive. "Uncle Dave's back! We gotta tell him!" Billy said quickly. "Go get him and tell him we have something to show him in the garden, just in case mom's there."

"Okay," Jake replied as he started running towards the front of the barn. "Be right back!" Within a minute, Jake reappeared around the corner with Uncle Dave right behind him.

"What's going on, Billy?" Dave asked. "Did you guys find those rabbit holes?"

Billy looked back past Dave to make sure his mother was coming. "No," he said in an excited half whisper. "We solved the map!" He held the piece of paper and waved it back and forth. Jake started dancing around, moving his head side to side.

"Are you kidding me?" Dave asked with a half grin on his face.

Billy began to explain. "Look right here!" He held a map up in front of Dave. Dave glanced down at the map as Billy continued. "Now look right up at the mountain. See the berry field? That's it! SM is SPRUCE MOUNTAIN and the square on the map is the blueberry field!"

"I don't believe it!" Dave exclaimed, staring back and forth between the map and the mountain. "How did you guys figure it out?"

"We were staring up at the mountain, thinking about going to get more blueberries for mom. Jake said it looks like a big old camels hump and that's exactly what I thought when I first saw the drawing on the map. Sure enough, it matched right up!"

Jake piped in, "We think that dotted line on the bottom is the brook because it goes all the way along the bottom of the mountain. MAYBE THERE'S BURIED TREASURE ON THE MOUNTAIN!"

"Quiet, Jake! Mom might hear you." Billy scolded as he stared at his brother.

"Too much of a coincidence not to be something," Dave replied. "Don't go getting all excited now. We do have a small problem coming up." Both boys looked over at him. "We have to tell your folks about this. If it really is something, they should know about."

Billy and Jake looked at each other with fear in their eyes. They were both thinking the same thing. "Dad's gonna' kill us," Jake said in a low voice as he stared at his brother.

"No he isn't," Dave assured them. "We'll tell him tonight. You just let me do all the talking. Don't say anything. Agreed?" The boys nodded in agreement as Dave turned to look back at the map. "I'm gonna' keep the paper for now. We've gotta get up there on the mountain to see if we can find something. It's too late tonight. Maybe tomorrow."

"Can't go tomorrow," Billy said quickly. "I'm going fishin with Timmy and his dad again over to Wilson Lake. It ain't fair we don't all go together."

Dave thought for a second. Billy was right. "OK, how about Sunday after lunch." He folded the paper and put it into his back pocket. "Let's get back to the house."

Supper finished up and Dave and Josh headed into the living room. Sophie and Billy finished up the dishes. It had been his turn to help. Billy came into the living room followed by Sophie. She was wiping her hands on a flowered apron that she had tied around her waist. Jake was playing with Bucky on the floor. "Don't get him all excited," she said to Jake. "You know what happens when you get him goin."

Cleo, the calico cat, was lying quietly on the floor next to Josh. She had become fairly friendly with the new pup. Moses, the large tomcat, wouldn't have anything to do with Bucky. Whenever the pup was around, Moses wasn't. Billy walked over and sat down next to Jake and Bucky on the floor. Sophie headed over towards the couch.

"Have a seat, Soph," Dave said patting the couch cushion. "I need to talk to you and Josh about something."

Sophie sat down as Dave leaned sideways and pulled the paper from his back pocket. He unfolded it and laid it on the small coffee table that sat in front of the couch. He proceeded to tell Josh and Sophie the story of how the boys had found both papers. They had shown this one to him but he told them to pay it no mind. He explained every detail, starting with Jake finding the jar right up to checking the mountain against the map earlier that afternoon. "The boys were going to tell you about it, but because I didn't think the papers meant anything, I told them they didn't have to tell you about them. I really didn't think there was anything to it, till the two of them figured out that the map was a drawing of Spruce Mountain. That's why I asked you about the initials SM the other night."

Josh looked over at the boys. He had always told them that they shouldn't keep secrets if they thought it was something important. They knew he was looking at them but they did not turn their heads. They kept staring right at Dave. Dave handed the paper to Sophie. She looked at it and then handed it to Josh. She had a look of amazement on her face. "You really think that it might have something to do with them robberies?" She asked.

"No idea," Dave replied. "All I know is that some of the things on the map match up with the mountain. I figured I'd take the boys up to the field on Sunday just to look around if that's okay with you."

"Huh," Josh mumbled. "Looks like someone drew up a picture ta show where tha blueberry patch was. Can't be much else to it."

"Probably not," Dave said. "Guess there is no harm in checking it out anyway. If we find anything we'll let you know right away."

"Sounds like a wild goose chase ta me," Josh said. "You boys betta git ta bed. Put that dog in tha kitchen fore ya go."

The boys got up, hugged their father around the neck and said good night to Dave. Bucky was put in the kitchen and Sophie followed the boys upstairs. Once she was gone, Josh looked over at Dave. "Ya really think there's sump-n' ta this paper?"

"I think it could be more than coincidence," Dave answered. "The first paper led to the second one that matches right up with the mountain and the blueberry field."

"Well, ya be careful with them boys up there. Once ya git past tha blueberry field them rocky areas can be pretty tricky. Don't need any of ya gittin' hurt."

"I'll keep a close eye on them for you. Don't worry," Dave assured him.

"Who's gonna' keep an eye on you!" Josh said with a loud laugh. Dave chuckled, folded the paper up and put it back into his pocket.

Later that evening as Dave lay in bed, he studied the map one more time. He looked at the letters and numbers on the top right, 3 TR and under that, 100 ft. He looked at the small lines along the top of the square that represented the blueberry field. The more he stared at it, the more he thought there was something familiar about it. Suddenly it hit him! When he was picking berries with the boys he had stopped to look at the landscape up towards the top of the mountain. He remembered the trees along the top edge of the field and the small stand of three trees clumped together on the top left side. His eyes widened. It looked just like the lines along the top of the square on the map. There were a few lines across the top and then a group of three at the top left. "3 TR," he said to himself. "Oh my God!" He said out loud. "3 TREES – it's the group of three trees. 3 TR, three trees, 3 TR, three trees," he kept saying over and over. The only thing left was the reference on the map to 100 ft. "Could be that whatever it is, it is located a hundred feet from the three trees," he said to himself.

He was actually starting to get excited about the possibilities. He wanted to get up and go up to the mountain right now! He couldn't believe that he was getting this excited over a piece of paper. "Calm down now Dave," he mumbled. "Can't let your imagination run wild on you." He folded the paper and put it on the small table next to the bed. He laid his head back on the pillow and let all the possible outcomes go rushing through his head. He fell asleep remembering something his father had always told him growing up. "NEVER ASSUME THAT THE OBVIOUS SOLUTION IS ALWAYS THE CORRECT ONE."

Billy was gone all day Saturday with Timmy and his dad. Dave and Jake went down to the store in the morning, and spent the rest of the day working around the house. Jake helped him out whenever he was not playing with Bucky or helping his mother with some chores.

Sunday arrived and turned into a complete disaster! They woke up to heavy rain and winds that were expected to last all day. After church, they went to visit their grandparent's over in Chesterville and had lunch with them. In mid-afternoon they returned home and spend the rest of the day indoors. There was no way they could go to the mountain in such bad weather. Dave and the boys talked a few times about the map and he told them about his three trees theory. He pointed to the lines on the map to show the boys where he thought the trees were. They would just have to wait until tomorrow to go check things out.

It was now Monday, August 19th. The boys would be starting back to school in just a couple of weeks. Sophie had already made plans to take them school shopping the following Saturday. Dave and the boys were anxious to get an early start up the mountain. The rain and winds had stopped during the night and the sun was up and bright this morning. They left the house at 9 am.

"You be careful up there and keep a close watch on them boys," Sophie told Dave as they were leaving the yard.

"I will, Soph, I will," he promised her.

They arrived at the blueberry field with only one minor incident. Jake had slipped on one of the rocks while crossing the brook. His shoe was waterlogged and his pants leg was wet all the way up to his knee. "That sun is really warm today. You'll dry out in no time," Dave said smiling at Jake.

Dave stopped as they entered the field and took out the paper. He stood there comparing the drawing to the landscape. The lines over the small square seemed to match the spruce trees that bordered the top of the field. He showed the boys and said, "Don't forget, this happened almost twelve years ago. There will be some new growth plus the original trees will be a little bigger." He pointed to the top left corner. "See those three spruce trees in the corner that are real close together? They match up with the three lines on the paper and the code 3 TR. We hope that means three trees. We're gonna' head up there and start looking around. Let's go!" They moved up through the field and headed towards the top left corner and the three spruce trees.

"Whatta we supposed to look for?" Jake asked as they approached the trees.

Dave shook his head. "I just don't know what we're looking for at this point. It could be a clump of dirt, a hole, or a pile of rocks. I just don't know. We just have to keep our eyes open for anything unusual. The paper says one hundred feet. Maybe it means one hundred feet from the trees. We can start with that. You might know I forgot to bring a tape measure."

"So how are we gonna' know how far one hundred feet is?" Billy asked.

"Okay, let's figure this out," Dave replied. "I have about a three foot stride. If I take thirty four paces it should be right around one hundred feet. Here's what we'll do. I'll walk straight up from the trees for thirty four paces. Then we'll stick a big branch in the ground to mark the spot. Then we'll do the same to the left side of the trees. Then we go to the right and last we'll walk down into the field. This will give us four markers, all one hundred feet out away from the trees." Dave knelt down and placed four little sticks on the ground to represent the markers. "Now if you could draw an imaginary curved line to connect all the markers, it would make a circle that was one hundred feet from the trees. Got it?"

"Hey! That's like when dad set up the garden out behind the barn. Except it was a rectangle not a circle," Jake stated.

"Exactly," said Dave. "We'll use the center tree as the starting point." He stood up against the tree and started pacing up towards the mountaintop. There wasn't much in front of him and he could see the rocks and ledge up ahead. He stopped at thirty four paces. The boys were right at his heels. "Okay, let's mark it."

Billy was carrying a broken branch from under one of the trees. They were still on solid ground with the rocky area just in front of them. Dave took a thin jagged rock and started digging a hole as deep as he could go. He set the end of the branch down into the hole and said to the boys, "grab some of those loose rocks and fill them in around this branch. That will help hold it in place." After they were finished with the placement of their first marker, they returned to the tree. They proceeded to measure out the other three markers in the same manner. The last one they did was down into the field.

"Now what?" Jake asked.

"Now we start looking." Dave stood by the marker and faced the marker to his right. He positioned the boys about four feet on each side of him. He started to explain what he wanted them to do. "We're gonna' walk from one marker to the next in a curved path. It's just like I showed you on the ground." He made a curved motioned with his hand pointing to the next marker. "Make sure we all stayed the same distance apart and just keep looking for anything unusual. Don't let anything go by. If you aren't sure, just yell "STOP" and we'll take a look at it. You boys ready?"

"I'm ready!" Billy yelled.

"Me too!" Jake echoed.

They started out with Dave setting a very slow pace. He would take a stride, stop, look around in all directions, stamp the ground, and take another step. Both Billy and Jake followed the same procedure until the first walk around was complete.

"Let's do a walk around in the opposite direction," Dave said as he moved in closer to the three trees.

The boys nodded in agreement but you could see from the expression on Jake's face that his interest in this search would soon be gone. "Okay," he said reluctantly.

They circled around at a faster pace and were back at the starting marker in about 15 minutes. "This is dumb. Just a wild goose chase like dad said," Jake complained.

"You might be right," Dave answered he looked around the area and up towards the rocky ledge that headed toward the top of the mountain. "If there's something out there, it could be anywhere. It could take a lifetime to find it."

They continued to walk around as the circles got smaller and smaller. They finally reached the three trees without any signs or discoveries.

"Can we go back now?" Jake whined. "I'm getting hungry."

"Yeah, sure. In a few minutes. You boys wait here by the trees. I'm gonna' check a bit more." Dave proceeded up towards the first marker. He continued past it until he was up into the rocky area. He took about five minutes to wander around, turning over some of the larger rocks and looking around the area. He came back and joined the boys. "Don't know where else to look right now. We'll study the map back at the house and see if we can come up with anything else. Let's go."

They arrived at the house around noon, hungry and frustrated. "I guess from the looks on your faces you didn't have to much success, huh?" Sophie said in a sympathetic voice.

The boys shook their heads. "Nope," said Dave. "We looked around everywhere. Thought we had a good clue from the paper but didn't find a thing." Dave sat down on the couch with the paper in his hand. Billy sat next to him. Jake headed out the door with Bucky. His interest in this mystery had all but disappeared. "Don't run off, Jake!" Sophie yelled. "I'm fixin lunch. It'll be ready in a few minutes!"

"I'll be right outside!" He yelled back.

Several minutes later they were all sitting at the kitchen table having lunch. Billy slapped the edge of the table and everyone looked over at him. He was sitting there shaking his head. "There's something there, I know it," he said emphatically. "How to figure out where it is, that's the question. Whoever drew that map had to make it real simple. We just can't figure it out." There was frustration in his voice.

"Don't get all upset, Billy," Sophie said. "Maybe it is simply like your dad said, just a drawin' of a blueberry field."

"I don't think so, Soph," Dave responded. "If that's all it was, why would it have initials and codes and footage on it? It's got to be something."

One More Try

After lunch, Dave headed out to the wood pile to chop more wood and calm his frustrations. Jake was playing with Bucky on the grass near the clothesline. Billy had wandered over to the old stump, sat down and was staring at the mountain. There were a million thoughts going through his head. "Hey, Uncle Dave!" Billy yelled over.

Dave brought the axe down hard and fast onto the chopping block and let go of the handle. Billy was walking toward him. "What's going on?" He asked as Billy approached him. Jake and Bucky started heading toward them.

"They taught us in the Boy Scouts that you should mark the area if you want to get back to a certain place. You know, we never did check out the trees to see if they had any marks."

"Billy, you might have something there," Dave said in a quick reply. "We've still got time this afternoon if you want to go back up and check it out."

Billy became excited. "Yeah, let's go!"

Before Jake could ask what was going on, Dave motioned towards the house and said, "Go tell your mother we're going back up to the mountain. GO, GO!"

Billy darted into the house while Jake stood there staring at his uncle. He could see that Uncle Dave was starting to get excited. "Do we really have to go?" Jake asked.

"You don't have to go if you don't want to. Don't you want to be there if we find something?"

"Yeah, I guess so," Jake said in a low toned voice.

Billy came back out of the door with Sophie close behind. "David, what's going on?"

"I can't explain now," he said hurriedly. "Billy had a notion about the area we checked and we got to go back up there," he said pointing in the direction of the mountain. "The boys will be fine with me. We shouldn't be that long."

"You know it's starting to get dark earlier now! You'll have to hurry to make it back before dark," Sophie stated.

"Got a flashlight just in case we need it?" Dave asked.

"Jake, run in and fetch the flashlight under the sink," Sophie said quickly.

Jake returned with the flashlight and held it towards Dave. "You carry it," Dave said as he darted over to the shed and grabbed a shovel. "Okay, let's get going."

"Please be careful!" Sophie yelled as they headed towards the pasture.

"We'll be fine!" Dave yelled back.

He looked over at the boys as they walked along. "We're on a fast pace here. You'll have to keep up." His long strides kept the boys in a slow trot. "Okay, let's review what we're going to do," Dave said as he walked along, swinging the shovel with each stride. "What's the first thing you're supposed to do when you're going out into the woods?" He asked Billy.

"Know where you're at and where you're goin'?" Billy questioned.

"That's right," Dave said. "And how do you get back?"

"Follow the trails," Jake answered quickly.

"What if there aren't any trails?"

"Then you should mark the trees so you can find your way back," said Billy.

"Exactly," Dave said. "Mark the trees so the mark points towards the location of the next mark, Right? That's pretty basic Boy Scout stuff. Just like you said back at the house, we never checked those trees for any marks or signs or nothing. I guess we were too busy looking for something on the ground."

They made it to the field in record time. Jake made it across the brook without getting wet. They were huffing and puffing as they reached the edge of the blueberry field. Dave knelt down on one knee. "Let's catch our breath for a few minutes. Then will head out to the trees." They reached the three spruce trees after taking a quick rest. "We're all gonna' check each tree," Dave said. "We're looking for some kind of mark or chunk out of the tree. Look for anything that someone could have made for a mark."

He leaned the shovel up against the middle tree. They each took a tree and started checking. As they slowly walked around the trees they searched up and down the barky trunks for any possible sign or clue. They took turns searching each of the three trees until they had completed all of them.

You could see the frustration on Dave's face. NOTHING FOUND! He had run the boys out here with the same results as the first time. He felt foolish. "You're a grown man getting all excited over nothing," he thought. "What an idiot I am!" He kicked at one of the trees in disgust, picked up a small rock and threw it towards the mountaintop. "WHY ARE YOU MAKING IT SO DIFFICULT FOR US!" he yelled, shaking his fist at the mountain. The boys could see that he was not happy with the situation.

"Maybe they marked one of them other trees," Billy said pointing to the other spruce trees along the top edge of the field.

Dave took a deep breath and tried to relax. He put his hands on his hips as he gazed down the row of trees. He recalled his father's words. "IT AIN'T ALWAYS THE OBVIOUS ONE!" He turned and said to Billy, "You know, I guess it wouldn't hurt to check them out since we're already here."

They started moving down the line of trees, circling each one and checking for any sort of signs or marks. After a while, Dave yelled down the line to the boys, "You guys find anything yet?"

"Nothin' here!" Billy yelled back as he continued to look up and down one of the trees.

"Nothin' down here either!" Jake yelled. "Just a nail stickin' outa this one."

Dave stopped quickly and looked down the row to where Jake was standing. "What was a nail doing in a tree in the middle of the mountain side?" He asked himself. "Billy, grab the shovel," he yelled as he ran down along the trees to where Jake was standing. "Where is it?" Dave asked excitedly as he looked at Jake.

"Where's what?" Jake asked not even aware that he may have found something important.

"The nail, Jake, the nail!" Dave yelled with a touch of frustration in his voice. "Sorry Jake, I didn't mean to yell at you," he said as he put his hand on Jake's shoulder. Jake pointed up along the trunk of the tree to a point about 7 feet high. A large rusty nail was sticking about 2 to 3 inches out of the trunk of the tree.

Billy joined them at the tree just as Dave reached up and touched the nail with his fingers. "Looks just like one of them big ones from that old can in the shed back at the house," Billy said.

"You're right!" Dave replied. "It does, doesn't it?" Dave looked around the area and back at the nail. They were much closer to the right side of the blueberry field. The rocky area and ledge were much closer than on the left side. He walked over and stood with his back up against the tree and his body position directly under the nail. He tilted his head back and looked directly up at it. He followed the direction that the nail head was pointing in with his eyes. It pointed right towards the mountaintop and the ledge area below it.

Dave pulled out the paper and looked at it again. He then stepped back from the tree and looked down the line. The tree that held the nail was the third tree in line from the right corner of the field. "N with the arrow! 3 TR, third tree from the right!" He yelled. "IT'S NEVER THE OBVIOUS ANSWER! Thanks dad."

"What's that mean?" Jake asked.

"Hopefully," Billy said, looking at Jake, "It means that the N with the arrow is the nail in the tree that points right towards the mountaintop. We gotta check it out to see if there's anything to it."

Dave stood under the nail one more time and lined the edge of the nail up with a point on the rocky area up ahead. He pointed out the spot he had picked and said to Billy, "You stand right here under the nail like I did." He then explained to Billy how to eye down the direction of the nail to see where it was pointing. "I'm gonna' walk off thirty four paces towards that spot. Just yell at me if I start to wander off to the left or right. Got it?"

"Okay," Billy replied.

"Jake, leave the flashlight here. Don't forget where you put it. Billy, let me under there one more time." Billy stepped aside and Dave realigned himself against the tree and started walking towards the ledge. Billy quickly took his position under the nail. Jake was following alongside Dave as he counted his paces. Dave had counted of twenty five paces when he heard Billy yell. He stopped and turned to look at Billy, keeping his extended foot firmly planted. Billy was motioning for him to move to the left. Dave made a half step sideways and looked back at Billy. Billy was giving him the thumbs-up sign.

Dave continued his count as he started forward. He was already into the rocky area and he could feel how loose some of the rocks were under his feet. He could see bigger slabs of rock and boulders ahead. He stopped again. "You stop right there," he said to Jake. "These rocks could get a bit tricky. Don't need you getting hurt. Your father would have my hide if anything happens to either of you."

Jake stopped and sat down on one of the rocks as Dave continued on. When he got to his thirty second step he was right up against a section of the ledge that protruded out from the side of the mountain. The ledge formed a small overhang in the shape of a V. He knelt down and looked in under the ledge. The opening went back in under about four to five feet. It was big enough for an animal or even a human to sit under if they needed a place to stay dry during a storm. He stood up and turned, putting his hands up in the air, and shrugged his shoulders to the boys. He waved for Billy to come up towards him. "Did I stay in line?" he yelled as Billy met up with Jake on the rocks below.

"Yeah, you were right even with it!" Billy yelled back. "Can we come up there?"

"Yeah, you gotta be real careful. Some of these rocks are really loose," he answered.

Billy and Jake inch their way towards Dave. When they got to the ledge, Dave was back on his knees, peering into the opening. It looked like a solid rock slab with a bunch of smaller rocks scattered all over it. "Sorry boys," Dave said in a disappointing voice. "Looks like another dead end."

"Knew I should have stayed home," Jake mumbled. "Nothin' but a waste a time."

Dave pointed in under the ledge. "It'll make a great hideout," he said, laughing and trying to break the gloom that had come over the boys faces.

Jake leaned in under the overhang to grab one of the small rocks. As the weight of his elbow came down on the rock slab, he felt it move. He jerked back quickly. "Did you see that?" He said in a startled voice.

"See what?" Billy asked.

"This thing just moved when I leaned on it," Jake said pointing to the slab. He leaned back in and pushed down on the slab with both hands. He felt it move again under his weight.

"Be careful there!" Dave said excitedly. "Let's clear all these rocks out of here, but be careful." They started grabbing the rocks and throwing them out behind them. The more they cleared, the more they could see that the slab was a long wide single piece that was lying under the ledge. All the rocks had been covering it to give the appearance that it was solid.

As they continued clearing, Billy noticed that some of the smaller stones near the back were disappearing down behind the slab and making a clicking sound. He stretched his arm in behind the slab and could feel a small opening along the back edge. "It feels like a opening back here!" He yelled.

Now they were all getting excited again, even Jake. Once all the rocks were removed it was easy to see the entire slab. It was obvious that it didn't belong under the ledge. "We gotta move it," Dave said to the boys. He positioned his body on the left end of the slab, reached in and grabbed the back side of it. Billy did the same on the right. They pulled outward but the slab was just too heavy. It didn't move an inch. Dave backed up and stood there staring at the slab.

"Hey, remember when dad had to move that old boiler out of the barn?" Billy said looking at Jake. "He used them small round logs to get under it and it rolled right out the barn door."

"Yeah, I remember that," Jake said. "So what?"

"That's a great idea, Billy," Dave replied. "Okay, here's what we'll do. We need a couple of sturdy round branches to pry it up, the stronger the better. And we need some long sturdy branches to lay under it once we get it lifted."

They headed toward the wooded area to look for branches that met Dave's requirements. The boys found several long round branches that fit the description. Dave went back to some of the larger trees and picked up two good-sized branches that were still solid. When they returned to the ledge, Dave wedged the first branch down and under the front left corner of the slab. "When I push down on it, you can stick the end of the one you have right in beside me as far as you can go," he instructed Billy. Dave inserted his branch down under the slab. He pushed down on the branch and as the slab lifted slightly, Billy stuck his branch down in alongside Dave's. Once they were in place, they were ready for the next task.

"Billy, you take hold of the front branch, I'll get the back one. When I say go, push down on the branch as hard as you can. It should lift the end of the slab right up. Jake, as soon as you see the slab lift up, stick those round branches straight in under. Make sure they go all the way across. OKAY, READY, GO!" Dave yelled.

Dave and Billy pushed down on the branches and the slab started to lift. Jake waited until it was high enough and slid the long round branches straight in under the slab. Once the branches were in place, Dave said, "Okay, Billy. Ease up on it." The slab settled back down on the branches that Jake had put in place. Dave and Billy pulled the two prying branches out away from the slab and tossed them aside.

"So far, so good," Dave said. "Let's hope the next thing works. Let's get over on the other side," he said pointing to the left end of the slab. "Since we can't stand up under there, we're gonna' have to sit down facing the end and push it with our feet. Those branches that Jake put under the other end should help us slide it right along. Jake, you're the smallest, so you slide in first, then Billy, then me."

They lined up side-by-side under the ledge with their knees bent up and their feet against the edge of the slab. "Okay," Dave said. "Let's all push on three. One, two, THREE!" As they all pushed together, the slab inched ahead about six inches and stopped. "Now what?" Dave muttered in a mad voice. He slid out and went to the other end of the slab.

They had missed clearing out some of the rocks that were off to the side and the edge of the slab had hit against them and stopped. He pulled the loose rocks out of the way, tossed them down the mountainside and returned to the boys. Once he was back in position, he said, "Let's try it again. One, two, THREE!" The second push slid the slab right over the hole and out the other side. Their hearts were racing.

They had uncovered a hole that had obviously been dug out. It was about 3 to 4 feet across the top and the sides were lined with thin flat pieces of rock. As they peered into the hole, they could see a dark green canvas looking material with a strap attached to it. "What do you think it is?" Billy yelled. "Do you think it's the money?"

"I don't know yet. Maybe, Maybe. Could be anything," Dave replied in a nervously excited voice.

Jake was making all sorts of weird faces, not knowing what to say. Dave motioned to the hole. "Let's see if you can get it out of there." Jake and Billy leaned in towards the hole and grabbed the green canvas on each side. They pulled in an upward motion but it wouldn't move. They tried again and still nothing happened. "You boys gotta move, so I can get it up out of there," Dave said as he motioned the boys out of the way.

Billy and Jake slid out from under the ledge and stood watching Dave. Dave laid his body alongside the hole, reached in and grabbed the strap and pulled it up. The material was loose as he started to lift it. Suddenly it tightened under his grasp. "It's some kind of sack," he said without looking at the boys. He continued wiggling and pulling at the sack until it began to gradually ease its way up. When it was almost to the top, he reached down and put his hand under the sack. With a quick final yank, it came up and out of the hole and came to rest alongside his body. Dave could see that the hole was fairly deep and had been lined on the sides and the bottom with the flat rocks. "Whoever did this knew exactly what they were doing," he said to the boys as he slid out from under the ledge.

He reached back in under, grabbed the sack on each side and pulled it out into the open area. "It's full of something," he said. "Let's get it back down by the trees. It'll be a little safer there."

The boys hurried around him as they headed back towards the field. Dave sat down next to the tree and Jake started yelling, "OPEN IT! OPEN IT!"

"It's a duffel bag," Dave told him. "Looks like an old Army one." He pointed to some faded black numbers stenciled along the outside of the bag. He turned it around to the other side. In the same black stencil lettering it read, "Pvt. Samuel Green." You could almost hear their hearts pounding as they stood there staring at the bag. Dave began to undo the straps across the top. He spread the top of the bag open and looked at Jake. "Go grab me the flashlight." Both his hands and his voice were shaking. He knew what he was going to find in the bag. Jake ran and grabbed the flashlight and brought it back to Dave. Dave was glancing around with a worried look on his face. "Oh no, I didn't even notice how late it was getting. The sun is already down behind the trees and it will be getting dark soon. We gotta hurry. It's gonna' get dark real quick."

Jake was hopping around, fingers crossed, trying to peek into the bag. "Do you see any money?" Billy asked. "What's in it?"

"It looks like another bag," Dave said as his trembling hand reached inside and grabbed the material. He lifted it out carefully. It was a folded up burlap bag, just like the one the cigar box had been wrapped in. "There's more of them down in there." Dave let go of the top of the duffel bag, knelt down and placed the burlap bag on the ground. He sat the flashlight down and started to unfold the bag. When he stuck his hand in and grabbed the contents, he knew immediately what he was holding. He paused for a second. His face had a look of excitement on it. The boys were kneeling next to him as he slid the contents out through the top of the bag and held it up in front of them.

"IT'S THE MONEY!" Jake screamed.

"IS IT REAL?" Billy yelled.

Dave leaned back against the tree, still holding it up in the air. It was a pack of $50 bills held together with a wide brown paper band. "There must be a thousand dollars right there! I can't believe we found it! I've never seen that much money in my life! You boys are gonna' be famous!"

"So are you, Uncle Dave!" Jake yelled. "Can we hold it?"

Dave nodded and handed them the pack of bills. "Of course you can, just be careful not to break it open," he said as he looked back into the burlap bag. There were at least 10 or 20 more packs plus some loose bills still remaining in the bag. He reached down in and felt around. There were two more burlap bags in the bottom. He felt deeper into the bottom and could feel some loose cloth. He grabbed onto one and pulled it up along the inside of the duffel bag and out through the top. It was a yellowish white bag that had "Farmington National Bank" written on the side. It was one of the money bags from the robberies.

Dave looked up quickly. Darkness was just about upon them. "Okay boys, we go to get this back to the house. We haven't got any time to spare. Look how dark it's getting." He took the pack of bills from Jake, put it back in the burlap bag and then stuck the burlap bag back inside of the duffel bag. He strapped the top back on, picked it up and slung it over his shoulder.

"Grab the flashlight, Billy, and don't forget the shovel, Jake. Billy, you lead the way. Let's get goin'."

Here Come the Police!

By the time they hit the brook, it was dark. Fortunately it was a clear night with a heaven full of stars and a bright moon that was giving them some extra light of its own. They were very careful crossing the brook, especially Jake. Once they had made it across, they headed for the pasture.

"What are we going to do with it?" Jake asked as they walked through the pasture.

"We're gonna' let the police know about it!" Billy blurted out.

"Yes, you're right. We've got to call the police as soon as we get back," Dave told them. "Let's not say anything until we get it all in the house, okay? I can't wait to see the looks on your folk's faces when we show them what we found. Your mom's gonna' kill me anyway. She's probably worried sick right now, wondering where we are. You know there is a reward for anyone who found this money. You guys are gonna' be famous, I tell you!" Billy and Jake started hopping side to side with their hands up in the air. Dave started laughing as Billy pushed Jake on the arm and smiled.

It was approaching 8:30 pm when they came up alongside the barn. Sophie was standing in the doorway and saw the shine from the flashlight. "Josh, there back!" She screamed as she burst out of the door and ran towards them. Her mouth was going a mile a minute. "Is everything okay? What happened? I was worried sick. Josh was gonna' call Fred and Skip to help go lookin' for you! Where's Jake and Billy?" She looked around and couldn't see them behind Dave.

"Everything's fine, Soph," Dave assured her.

"I'm right here, mom," Jake said as he ran out from behind Dave. "Guess what? We found......AH..... A nail in a tree." He remembered he was not supposed to say anything until they were in the house.

"We're running a little bit late," Dave piped in. "We had a great time, huh, boys?" They both nodded in agreement.

"What do you have there?" Sophie asked pointing to the bag on Dave's shoulder.

"Let's get in to the house and we'll tell you all about it," Dave said.

They headed for the house. Josh was standing in the doorway, obviously not as excited or worried as Sophie. "Told ya they were fine," Josh said to Sophie as she passed through the doorway. She curled her mouth up a bit but didn't answer. Dave and the boys followed her in. "We thought them bears mighta had ya fa suppa," Josh said laughing. Sophie just stood there shaking her head. Josh was curiously eyeing the bag as Dave set it down on the living room floor.

"You two better sit down, we've got something to show you," Dave said motioning Sophie and Josh to their seats.

Josh took up residence in his big old chair and Sophie walked over and sat down on the couch. The boys were fidgeting around as Dave started to open the duffel bag. Bucky was jumping up on Jake's leg, trying to get him to play. Dave reached into the duffel bag, fumbled around inside to get the pack of bills out of the burlap bag, and pulled it out. "Catch!" He yelled, as he tossed the pack of bills at Josh.

Josh caught it like it was too hot to handle. His mouth was hanging open as he looked at the pack of bills. Sophie screamed, "Oh my Lord. Is that money?"

"Sure is," Billy boasted.

"Well, I'll be damned!" Josh bellowed out in amazement. "I don't believe it. How much is it?" Sophie didn't even respond to his cussing. She was so amazed, she couldn't even speak.

"We didn't count it all. But there are three burlap bags inside this duffel bag plus a bunch of empty money bags in the bottom. I don't think we should pull it all out. We can let the cops do that," Dave said. "The duffel bag belonged to Sam

Green, one of those fellas that were shot here at the house." Dave pointed to the lettering on the side of the bag.

Sophie just sat there, lost for words. Dave and the boys proceeded to tell the entire events of the afternoon leading up to finding the money. When he finished, Dave said, "Josh we need to call the police and get someone up here."

"NOW?" Sophie blurted out. "It's nine o'clock at night." She glanced over at Josh.

"Beta call tha Sheriff's Department ova in Farmington," Josh said to Dave. "See if ya can git holda Tommy Stiles. Think he's one a them detective fellas ova there."

"You know him?" Dave asked Josh.

"Yes sa. Went ta school with em."

"Well, maybe you should call him," Dave replied.

"Guess I kin." Josh stood up and headed for the phone that sat on a small table near the corner. It was one of those new dial phones that had just been installed this year. He pulled a small phone book out of the book rack and looked up the number. "GS42625," he said repeatedly as he jotted it down on a small piece of paper. He picked up the phone and dialed the number. After a few rings, a voice answered on the other end. "Sheriff's Department, can I help you?"

"Hope so," Josh answered. "I'm tryin' ta git a holda Tommy Stiles. Any chance he might be there?"

"Not tonight, sir. But you should be able to get him in the morning, around nine am," came the response.

"Maybe I'll try em at home. Thanks, bye." Josh hung up the phone and started looking through the phonebook again. "Stiles, Stiles, Thomas," he mumbled until he found the listing. He jotted down the number then dialed once more and waited. A man's voice came on the other hand. "Hello."

"Tommy, this is Josh Baka up on Macomber Hill in North Jay."

"Hi, Josh, I ain't talked to you in a long time," Tommy said.

"Ya still with the Sheriff's Department ain't ya?" Josh asked.

"I sure am. What's going on?"

"You remember them robberies that happened bout eleven years ago? They shot them two fellas right up hea on tha 'Hill'." Josh stated.

"Yes I do. I was working on that case for a while after it all happened." Tommy responded.

"Well," Josh continued. "We got some stuff up hea that's tied in with them robberies. Figured someone might want ta come up en take a look."

"What do you have up there Josh?" Tommy asked inquisitively.

"I think we got all that money they stole," Josh answered. There was a dead silence on the other end of the line. "Hey, Tommy! Ya still there?"

"Yeah, I'm here," Tommy said hurriedly. "Are you serious, Josh? You ain't pulling my leg, are you?"

"Nope," Josh chuckled. "Wouldn't do that. Sides you ain't hea fa me ta pull it anyways. We got some big bags a money hea so ya might want ta git up hea fore we go out en spend it all."

"Okay, okay Josh," Tommy said seriously. "You can't go spending any of it, you know that?"

"I'm just kiddin' with ya," Josh replied jokingly.

"About the money?" Tommy asked.

"No, no, that's fa real. I mean bout spendin' it. Kin ya come or not?"

"Okay, I need to make a couple of calls first," Tommy said. "But we should be there in an hour or so."

"K, see ya then," Josh answered. He shook his head as he put the phone back on the hook. "Darn fool thought I was really gonna' spend tha money," he mumbled as he put the phone book away.

Everyone had been listening to Josh while he was on the phone. He turned and looked at them. "They'll be hea in bout an hour," he said. He walked over and sat down in his chair. He was still chuckling. "I can't believe he thought I might go spend some a that money!" He said looking at Dave. Dave shook his head and laughed.

"We can stay up, right mom?" Billy asked in a pleading voice.

"Well, all right. Only because it's such a big deal," Sophie responded.

They sat there talking about everything while waiting for Tommy to arrive. The boys kept looking at the rooster clock in the kitchen. It seemed like forever for that hour to go by. Finally they heard a car pull into the yard. They heard two car doors close, then came the knock on the door. Dave got up and said, "I'll get it." He walked over and opened the door and said, "Come on in."

Two men entered the house. The first man was Tommy Stiles. The second followed him in, carrying what looked like a small leather suitcase. "Tommy, it's good ta see ya," Josh said as he reached out to shake Tommy's hand. "This here's my brother in law, Dave Clough." Tommy reached over to shake Dave's hand. "My wife Sophie en my two boys, Billy en Jake," Josh continued as he pointed them out.

"This is Bob Tibbetts," Tommy said pointing to the man that came in with him. "He works for the department." Everyone said their greetings and hello's to Bob. "He's gonna' be taken some pictures, if you got what you say you got," Tommy remarked.

"Oh, we got it," Josh said smiling. "Right ova hea."

Dave walked over towards the couch as the rest of the group followed. He cleared off the coffee table in front of the couch. As he knelt down, he opened the end of the duffel bag and pulled out the first burlap bag. He unfolded it, set it on the coffee table, reached in and pulled out the first pack of bills. "There's a lot more where that come from," he said as he handed the bills to Tommy. "Two more burlap bags inside this one and a bunch of empty money bags in the bottom too!"

Tommy and Bob stood there staring at the money. Dave handed Tommy one of the empty money bags from the Farmington National Bank. He proceeded to hold open the top of the burlap bag. You could see the other packs of money inside. "There are a few loose bills thrown in here too," Dave said.

"This is unbelievable!" Tommy gasped. "I don't think anyone ever thought we'd ever see this money again! Hope you don't mind, but I'm gonna' have to get a bunch of information from you."

Tommy sat and listened while Dave and the boys told their story one more time. He listened intensely and took pages and pages of notes. Meanwhile, Bob had taken a camera out of his black suitcase. He removed the rest of the money from the first burlap bag and set it on top of the bag on the table. He removed the other two burlap bags from the duffel bag and place them next to the money that was on the table, but did not open them. Finally, he pulled out some of the empty money bags and laid them out so that you could read the names of the banks that were on them. Everyone else was listening to Dave and the boys retell their story.

Suddenly there was a big flash! Sophie screamed and almost jumped off the couch. "Sorry," Bob said apologetically. "I'll give you a warning when I take the next one." He smiled his apology at Sophie.

Dave and the boys continued on with their story, in amongst Bob yelling, "Picture time!" every time there was going to be a flash. "Looks like this duffel bag belonged to Sam Green," Bob said as he took some pictures of it.

"Dave mentioned that already," Tommy responded. Bob just nodded. By the time they finished it was almost midnight. Bob had packed up his camera, put the money back into the burlap bag, loaded everything back into the duffel bag and strapped it shut.

"We've got to take all this back to Farmington. I already called some other people before I came," Tommy said. "There's gonna' be a lot more of them involved in this by morning. They'll probably be back over here by eight am. You should all be here because there's gonna' be a lot more questions and they're gonna' want to talk to all of you. Just don't tell anyone about it yet. This is a big event, A REAL BIG ONE!" He said emphatically.

"Someone said that there is a reward for finding it, is that true?" Billy asked.

"Oh yes," Tommy said shaking his head in agreement. "I'm sure they'll tell you all about it tomorrow." Tommy and Bob gathered everything up and carried it out to the car. They put the duffel bag in the trunk, backed out of the yard and headed for Farmington.

"That's just too much excitement for anyone," Sophie stated as they all headed up to bed. "Just too much! You boys get to bed now. We'll see you in the mornin'."

Billy and Jake were exhausted from the long day of activities but were too excited to fall right asleep. "Are we really gonna' get some money for findin' all that?" Jake asked Billy.

"Think so," Billy replied. "Mr. Stiles said that there's a reward for findin' the money."

"Wonder how much. Maybe Fifty Dollars!" Jake said excitedly.

"Maybe a Hundred!" Billy answered back. "Now let's get to sleep." The boys finally drifted off to sleep thinking about the money, the reward and the events of the day.

Josh got up at his usual time, around 3:45 am. He had his breakfast and drove to the dairy, still a bit tired from the short night's sleep. He would help Fred and Skip get through the morning milking. He informed them upon his arrival that he had to return home around 7:30 for some personal business and as soon as he was done with it, he would return to the dairy. He remembered that Tommy had asked them not to say anything about what was going on yet. When the milking was done and Josh was getting ready to head back to the house, he told Fred and Skip, "If Everett comes out lookin' fa me, tell em I'll explain everything to em when I git back."

Sophie, Dave and the boys had already finished up breakfast and were putting the dishes away in the kitchen when Josh entered the house. At five minutes past eight, a parade of cars, six in all, headed up Macomber Hill. As they crested the hill, they turned and pulled up into the driveway. There were two County Sheriff's cars, two State Police cars, a long black Buick and a white Ford. The Buick carried an agent from the FBI office down in Augusta and the white Ford belonged to a reporter from the Farmington Gazette.

Tommy Stiles and Bob Tibbetts were the first two out. They were followed by two more members of the sheriff's department, two State Police officers, the FBI agent and the reporter. Josh was already holding the door open and ushered them all in as they approached. Tommy proceeded to make all the quick introductions.

"Ya lookin' a little tired, Tommy," Josh said putting his hand on Tommy's shoulder.

"You too, Josh. Bob and I have been up all night making reports, counting money and calling all these people to let them know what was going on."

"How much money was it!" Jake blurted out.

"Hush, Jake!" Sophie scolded.

"That's okay," Tommy said. "It was quite a bit. He started smiling. "We totally it up to be about a hundred thousand dollars, give or take a few pennies," he said with a little laugh.

Sophie gasped. Dave, Billy and Jake stood there, wide-eyed, not believing what they had just heard. Josh dropped his hand from Tommy shoulder. "This just ain't real. Must be a dream," he said shaking his head.

Everyone was smiling. "It's no dream, sir," the FBI agent said. "You folks have made quite a find here. This was a federal crime. There's a five thousand dollar reward for finding all this money."

The room became totally silent. "It----- it was my two boys en their uncle who found it," Josh acknowledged pointing towards them.

"No, no," Dave said quickly. "It was the boys who solve the whole thing. They should get it!"

"It doesn't matter right now," said the agent. "We can figure out all those details later."

"Well," Tommy broke in. "All these people need to hear your stories about how you found it. So we better get on with it. Dean's gonna' be takin' some pictures for the paper, if that's okay?"

"Sure," Josh replied.

Each of the men questioned and took notes, one at a time. Billy, Jake and Uncle Dave told them their versions of the story. Sophie and Josh just answered some general questions since they had not become involved until the very end of the discovery. Tommy was telling Josh and Sophie how they still believed that there had been three people involved in the robberies. "That money was all counted out into three separate bags. There was thirty five thousand each in the first two and almost thirty thousand in the third. We figured that the two that got shot had split it up into the bags, then hid it. We must have gotten to them before they had a chance to tell the third fella where they had put it. We never found any clues as to who the other fella could have been or if there really was one. The stories say that there was a getaway driver but that's all just a guess on our part."

The questions and stories finally came to an end. Dean got the family together on the couch and took several pictures for the paper. He took several of the entire family and then took some more of just Dave and the boys. When he finished, Tommy said, "Now we need to take a walk up to the mountain. We need to see where you found it. Everything has to be verified for the record."

"Ya don't need me along, do ya?" Josh asked. "I gotta git back ta tha dairy. Kin I tell Mr. Robinson what's goin on?"

"Sure, that's fine," Tommy responded. "Dave and the boys can take us up. You can tell anyone you want now. It'll be all over the state by tomorrow." He pointed to Dean from the newspaper.

One by one, they headed out into the yard. "Sophie, you're welcome to come along too!" Tommy yelled as they headed towards the pasture.

"Oh no!" She yelled as she waved to them. "I'd rather stay right here! Bucky can keep me company."

He waved back his acknowledgment and then continued on with the group. Josh had his arm around Sophie's shoulder. As he kissed her cheek, he said, "Mrs. Baka, ain't that tha damnedest thing that eva happened?"

"Josh Baker!" She said with that scolding look. Then she started laughing and shaking her head. He let go of her shoulder and headed for his car, whistling Hank Williams, "I Saw The Light". "See ya later," he said as he waved to Sophie and headed for the dairy. It was almost 10 am.

When he arrived at the dairy he headed straight for the house. He stepped through the porch doorway and knocked on the inside door. Everett opened the door. When he saw Josh, he asked, "Everything okay, Josh? The boys told me ya had to go home for a bit. Come on in." Josh followed Everett into the dining room. As he entered, he could smell the stench of heavy cigar odor throughout the house.

"I'm runnin' a bit late taday, Everett. You just ain't gonna' believe what's goin' on." Josh proceeded to tell him all the events that had taken place right up through this morning. When he finished, he said, "I just wanted ta let ya know what was goin' on, that's all."

Everett was standing there shaking his head. "Ain't that crazy, Josh. Just crazy!" He remarked.

"Who's out there, Ev?" said a voice from the other room.

"It's Josh, come out and say hello Carl!" Everett yelled.

The doorway of the living room was in the back and off to the right. It filled to capacity as Carl Robinson made his way through it and into the dining room. He did not look in good health and required two canes to help him maneuver his way through the house. "Howdy, Josh," Carl said in a low raspy voice.

"Josh was just telling me that the boys and Sophie's brother found all that money that was stolen in them bank robberies way back eleven years ago. You remember that?"

Carl made his way over to a small table that sat against the wall on the right side of the room. In the middle of the table sat a small dark brown wooden cigar box with a big gold label that read, "GARCIA – HAVANA". He leaned one of his canes against the table, reached down and opened the box and took out a cigar. He stuffed the cigar in his shirt pocket and picked up his cane. "HUH! Ain't no concern a mine." He grunted. He turned, waved one of his canes at Josh and headed back into the other room.

"Don't pay him no mind. He don't have much concern bout nothin', these days." Everett turned his head towards the other room. "Ain't that right, TINY!" He yelled to Carl. Carl gave no response back.

Josh looked in towards the living room. "Well..... I guess I betta git out ta tha barns," he said rather nervously.

"Okay, thanks for lettin' me know," Everett replied.

Josh headed down the porch steps and towards the barns. Callie, the barn cat, came running towards him. As he approached the milk house, he stopped, reached into his pocket and removed a piece of paper. It was the first piece of paper that Jake had found in the cellar. Josh had found it a while back in the barn at the house. As he smoothed it out, he read the top line: "Share", Then he gazed down to the third line: "TINY – 30".

"Well I'll be!" He said out loud, glancing back at the house. He shook his head from side to side and headed towards the barns. "Tiny, huh," he mumbled to himself. "Now that's a nickname that sure fits! Josh knew that "TINY" only had a month or two left to live so he decided that he would keep this information to himself.

He opened the barn door and entered, singing his favorite Hank Williams tune, "I'm So Lonesome I Could Cry", with Callie right on his heels. He crumpled up the paper and tossed it in a bucket by the wall. As the door closed behind him, he looked up at the small plaque on the wall that read, "Josh Baker, Dairyman of the Year, 1957".

Summer's End

It was Saturday, September 21st, the first day of fall, but what a summer it had been. The boys had been back to school since just after Labor Day. They were local heroes and were asked over and over again to tell their story.

The Farmington Police Department had held a ceremony to thank the boys for solving the money mystery. The FBI agent from Augusta was there and presented them with the reward money. It was a check for FIVE THOUSAND DOLLARS! Billy and Jake wanted the money to be for the whole family, including Uncle Dave.

Josh was able to get rid of his beat up Pontiac and buy a brand new 1957 Buick. He had always liked the Buick, but could never afford a new one. Dave was given a share of the reward money and the rest was put into bank accounts for Billy and Jake. Sophie and Josh were hoping that the boys would be able to use it for their future education.

Josh had been able to get in another small haying session just before the weather started getting cooler. He informed Jake that he could start helping out at the dairy because of the great job he did at the fair. Dave found a job as a machinist over in Farmington and had finally gotten up the courage to ask Anne, from the library, out on a date. They have been seeing each other ever since.

Today was a cool day even though the sun was shining bright. Billy and Jake were outside playing with Bucky. Billy walked over to the old stump on the front lawn and sat down facing Spruce Mountain. He kept staring at the small opening of the field on the mountain and picturing the map in his mind. Over a month had gone by since the discovery and he still couldn't believe everything that had happened. "What a summer on the 'Hill' this has been," he thought to himself. "Wonder what adventures the winter will bring." He crossed his legs on the stump, leaned his head back, and closed his eyes. Jake had been chasing Bucky over near the clothesline. He quickly snuck up behind Billy and stuck his finger into Billy's ribs. Billy jumped as Jake yelled, "LOOK OUT FOR THEM ROBBERS!" Jake took off running towards the barn with Billy chasing him. Bucky was right behind them.

Billy yelled at Jake, "You're gonna' pay for that one!"

Jake started to make the sound of a cackling chicken as he rushed into the barn.

Billy continued running after him, yelling, "CUT IT OUT!"

About the Author

John was born in Farmington, Maine in April of 1948. He lived in Chesterville, North Jay, and Limerick through the age of ten. His family moved to New Hampshire when he was in the fifth grade. He joined the Air Force in 1966 and served a one year tour in Vietnam from 1968 to1969. He worked in the computer industry for twenty years and owned several small businesses. He retired from the federal government on his birthday in 2014. He is an avid genealogist and has spent many years building his family history with his sister, Marcia. John and his wife, Linda, relocated to Milo, Maine in July of 2014 and currently reside there.

Made in the USA
Middletown, DE
11 June 2016